Untruly Yours

Smita Shetty

FROG BOOKS

First published in India 2012 by Frog Books
An imprint of Leadstart Publishing Pvt Ltd
1 Level, Trade Centre
Bandra Kurla Complex
Bandra (East) Mumbai 400 051 India
Telephone: +91-22-40700804
Fax: +91-22-40700800
Email: info@leadstartcorp.com
www.leadstartcorp.com / www.frogbooks.net

Sales Office:
Unit: 122 / Building B/2
First Floor, Near Wadala RTO
Wadala (East) Mumbai 400 037 India
Phone: +91-22-24046887

US Office:
Axis Corp, 7845 E Oakbrook Circle
Madison, WI 53717 USA

Copyright © Smita Shetty

ISBN 978-93-81836-29-3

Book Editor: Gunjan Verma
Design Editor: Mishta Roy

Typeset in Book Antiqua
Printed at Repro India Ltd, Mumbai

Price — India: Rs 125; Elsewhere: US $5

Dedication

For my son and in memory of my loving father.

About the Author

Smita Shetty has been in the creative field for over seven years. In her spare time she enjoys involving herself in community work. She offers her creative support to Gujarat Hindu Society and has taken up several designing projects for a County Council's employee network group. *Untruly yours* is her debut novel. Smita is originally from Mumbai, India and currently lives with her family in the United Kingdom.

Acknowledgements

I would like to express my deepest gratitude to my friend Geetu Purkayastha for twisting my arm to get me writing, Andy Winters for putting up with the unenviable task of proof reading every chapter even when he was quietly busy project leading multiple assignments including writing his own children's book, my dear mother for her infectious strength and resilience, my sister Niketa Shetty for always being there for me, my precious friends Divya Amarnani, Nupur Poddar and Sonia Bharadwaj, for laughing uproariously at my silliest anecdotes.

And finally, my earth angels - Charu Ainscough and Ayesha Madan, for their unstinting love and support.

Dearest Ayesha...

with love

Sni x

Chapter One

'That's it Mum keep going, you are doing a grand job!' I hear 'the son's' patronizing voice behind me. I look back at him and smile weakly, unable to take the admiring remark with more enthusiasm.

I thought it was quite clever of me to trick him into assisting me to tackle our garden that had slowly begun to resemble the Amazonian rainforest. I had lured him in, promising him a jolly day of bug watching and planting his dud seeds (given away free in junk catalogues). Gardening doesn't exactly fill me with joy and I enjoy it even less when I have to do it on my own.

A few minutes ago, we had refuelled ourselves with an extra cup of tea and hot chocolate, bracing ourselves for a long and laborious day ahead. So, there we were, me armed with a blunt shovel and Rishab, my son, with an ill-fitting pair of garden gloves. Although the gloves were a year old they were never put to much use which explained the state of the garden.

I felt like a proud mum, spending 'quality' time with her only child. We made a pretty picture, the two of us, ready to take on the world. We took a deep breath, filling puffed lungs with oxygen-rich air, gave a brief encouraging smile to each other and started digging out the 'killer' weeds with vengeance. I never quite understood how these annoying botanical species grew in the first place. They creep in everywhere, between slate titles, bricks, stones and you name it. They grow at an astounding rate; it's almost like you've secretly fed them with plant feed. Only if they were a tad prettier, I wouldn't have had the mammoth task of painstakingly digging them out come spring-summer.

'Mum, look what's happened to our Jasminum Fucticans!' Rishab screeched and shuddered in shock horror as he pointed at a bundle of dried twigs.

Jasminum Fructicans! Dear lord! This child never fails to freak me out. It's not always easy being around a human Wikipedia. 'Jasmine' would have done just fine. I quickly blamed the premature demise of the foliage on poor soil quality and the clueless son nodded solemnly.

We'd only just gotten over our minor setback, when I heard an earth shattering sneeze. Chances of it being a pretend one seemed high. It was Rishab's way of throwing in the towel. With Rishab, when the going gets tough 'he' gets going. It didn't take him long to realise that he'd much rather be doing something else. With one miserable weed attached to one of the garden gloves; he made his polite and blatantly fraudulent excuse, 'Mum, I think it's the hay fever. Can I watch you from a distance? I don't want to be sick again.'

Well, I couldn't take a chance on that, could I? Especially, when the poor soul suffers from eczema as well. 'That's okay darling, off you go. I'll see you in a bit.' *That's if these blooming weeds don't kill me.*

Rishab does stick to his words this time. He watches me from a distance, necking down umpteen glasses of cold pink lemonade, while I dodge different species of spiders and bugs. I hear him chuckle every time my shorts slip from my hips as I get engrossed and lean further more to dig out the strong roots. I choose to ignore him. I mean, is there a dignified position for a serious gardener? But before I can lose the will to live, I call it a day.

I stagger back into the house when Rishab offers to make me a glass of his infamous pink lemonade. The drink is a concoction of lemon, water, sugar, pink food colouring, mixed with a generous helping of Rishab's germs. This child never remembers to clean his hands. I politely decline the kind offer and just as I find my strength to smile, I take a brief look around the kitchen. I can't find my voice to let out one of my blood curdling shrieks. These shrieks are often due to the result of cheeky chops' efforts to demolish the house by not cleaning up after himself. Rishab in a matter of minutes has turned the kitchen into a war zone. The cabinet doors are swung open, exposing the orderly arranged spice jars and glass bottles containing every dry mandatory cooking ingredient that's ever been made available for us 'cheffy' types. The sugar jar which should be one amongst them is on the worktop with its lid flung open. Every inch of the kitchen is covered with large and small pools of water. I doubt whether he'd been engaged in a water fight with his imaginary friend.

'Rishab, why do you do this to me? Can't you ever put things back in its place? And why are there fingerprints on the sugar jar?' I interrogate hysterically. I often wondered if I am ever taken seriously by my demolition spawn. Lessons are never learnt. And Rishab slips back into his old ways again in no time.

'Oh here she goes again, Mrs Hygienic!' he shakes his head and complains to his imaginary friend.

I hate it when he talks to me in third person.

I decide I need some carbohydrates in my body before I explode. I'd just embarked on an ambitious stringent diet, inspired lately by waif like actresses in *Desperate Housewives*. I had devised my very own three-step bespoke diet. Starve, shrink the stomach and introduce bits of food intermittently to keep me from passing out. However, the plan was wearing thin. It was day two and Rishab's chubby hands were looking particularly enticing.

'Mum!' the son roars like an army general, as I reach for a bag of chips. *Damn! I'd forgotten I had put Rishab in charge to keep me in check.* 'You are impossible! I can't take my eyes off you for one minute,' Rishab wags a reproving finger and snatches the chips packet from me and starts munching the contents noisily. I could tell he is enjoying the powers I had foolishly bestowed upon him. 'Stay strong Mum...you are doing really well,' he says, patting my bulging belly. *Yet another patronizing praise.* With that parting shot he shuffles out of the room leaving a trail of chip flakes behind him.

This child is slowly ageing me; I am a 36 years old woman going on 60. Of late, I have been experiencing all the vital symptoms associated with ageing – dementia, angina and even hair loss! Every time I enter his room, a clump of hair hits the floor. But

I wouldn't trade him for anyone else in the world. Apart from keeping the house tidy and shopping, we agree on almost everything. We are one unit. Two peas in a pod. Rakesh, my husband chooses to believe Rishab is his daddy's little boy. We let him believe it's true.

Rakesh and I studied in the same college in Mumbai for two years. Although we were in the same class, I didn't know he'd even existed until one fateful day of our second year. We were in our chemistry laboratory in the midst of performing the most pointless experiment - Charcoal cavity test, to identify a mineral. I dreaded our chemistry laboratory; it was full of foul smelling chemicals stored in grubby glass jars, all randomly arranged and incorrectly labelled. We considered ourselves blessed if we found one undamaged test tube to work with. The blowpipes which were meant to have two holes, one on each end, had more holes than one could imagine. The Bunsen burners would burn when you would least expect them to. On this particular occasion it performed its functions rather well. It set fire to my lab coat.

It was one of many mortifying moments of my life. I was completely unaware of the drama behind me as I struggled to blow the flame into the cavity. Although I must admit it was unusually quiet for a bit. Folks behind me had lost their voice as they watched my lab coat go up in flames, with me still wearing the damn thing. Rakesh gallantly came to the rescue. He launched himself on me and stripped off the blazing lab coat.

I was paralyzed for a moment when I'd swung my head around to make sense of it all. Behind me were horrified fellow students all huddled together. Some had turned to stone. We'd all stood silently watching a scrawny teen perform a wild tribal jig over my coat in an attempt to put out the flames. The teen displaying some serious hip-action, was about average height bearing in mind, he still had a few years left in his kitty to grow another inch or two. It didn't take me long to gather my thoughts and piece together what had just transpired.

'Are you okay, Natasha?' I heard Professor Patil's unmistakable high pitched nasal voice. 'You should be more careful. You were meant to direct the flame into the cavity and not your lab coat!'

he chuckled loudly at his own joke. I failed to find any humour in it unlike the rest of the class.

'I am so embarrassed. Just when I think I can't embarrass myself anymore, I go and surprise myself. Who is this guy Priti?' I'd enquired with my lab partner and best friend.

'You can't be serious! Natasha honestly, you're always away with the fairies,' Priti had said exasperated and wishing she wasn't lumbered with a scatty friend-for-life. 'Rakesh has been with us since the last year!' Priti explained wearily like I was meant to know these things. Rakesh was an average, regular teenager. He didn't exactly stand out of the crowd so how was I supposed to know him unless we had been introduced to each other.

'Uh right! I'd best go and thank him,' I said, somewhat shamefaced and not quite getting over the recent embarrassment.

From the time we'd introduced ourselves, we'd been inseparable.

Chapter Two

Rakesh and I may have been inseparable, but decided to go our separate ways academically. He had aspired to study medicine and I aspired to have pure unadulterated fun. He got great grades that year and secured admission into one of the most prestigious medical colleges in India. I continued my education in the same institute and went on to achieve Masters in Microbiology. Why I opted to study Microbiology still remains a mystery.

I may have missed Rakesh studying with me but in a way I liked the space between us. I got more time to spend with my friends - Priti, Diya, Veer and Sanjay. And Rakesh got more time to spend with his new found medical buddies to discuss joys of dissecting mummified corpses with sheer precision. While I couldn't be bothered with the company he was keeping, Rakesh seemed extremely disturbed with my choice of friends. And my friends never understood what made us tick as a couple.

Priti tried very hard to accept us as a couple. Although she had never mentioned why she disapproved of me going out with Rakesh, I suspect she found Rakesh overtly possessive about me. Priti and Rakesh didn't quite hit it off. She could never get past saying 'Hey Rakesh, how is it going?' And whoosh she was gone, not waiting to even find out what Rakesh had to say about his day. Rakesh found this quality about her most infuriating.

I shared a special bond with Priti as we had been friends since the time we were in school. She was a chubby little girl with greasy pigtails. She wore a uniform that was always a size smaller which didn't do much justice to her round body. She would find endless innovative ways to put her school tie to use like cleaning her nose when she suffered from a bad cold, nibbling on loose threads when she got hungry or nervous, wiping beads of sweat on a hot humid day and the corners of her mouth after a meal or a drink. Personal hygiene clearly didn't rate very high on her list of priorities. But she made me smile. She was the brightest girl in class and it didn't come as a surprise when she chose me to be her best mate.

She came from a very affluent, rigid, orthodox Punjabi family. Being a naturally free spirited girl, it wasn't easy for Priti to grow up in a conservative family especially when her big brother was even more domineering and protective than her father. Her brother Neeraj, studied in the same school and college as us, which made life more difficult than it already was for Priti. They had two years between them. But I am sure it felt like twenty. It was as if the only mission in his life was to spy on Priti. If she stood talking to a boy for more than a few seconds she could hear him breathing over her shoulder in no time. As if that wasn't enough, his friends had even volunteered their 'services' to keep a check on their friend's little sister's movements. She would have an entourage following her everywhere during lunch or play time. It was deeply unsettling at first but we soon got used to them.

The entourage had grown in size as Priti grew prettier with each passing year. Thankfully, she took pride in her appearance. She was the official eye candy of our college. She no longer rolled or wobbled, instead she walked with elegance and confidence. As Priti was showing the world how steering clear of chocolates, chips and her mother's grease-laden food can give tangible results, her parents were frenetically hunting for prospective grooms for the oblivious soul. They didn't take long to find her a perfect soul mate.

The prospective groom, Deepak, belonged to an equally affluent and orthodox Punjabi family. Priti's and Deepak's parents who came from traditional families decided that their children would find love and happiness with grooms and brides of their choice. How refreshingly novel! Whatever happened to love, courtship and romance?

Priti was only eighteen when she first met Deepak. Priti did try to protest and stand up to her father. Her father then began enlightening her about marriages that were arranged during his time, when *their* society was not as liberal minded as him (!) Families of the bride and the groom arranged marriages and the couple met only at the time of the ceremony. In other words, she should count herself lucky, because she was given the opportunity to see her groom before marriage! Seeing no way out of the situation and bored to tears about stories of her father being broad minded, she agreed to meet Deepak on two conditions - a) she gets to turn down the 'chosen one' if she didn't like him and b) she wanted me, her best mate, the one who was almost joint to her hip, to be there with her. It was my turn to protest. But before I could say 'No way Jose,' I found myself at Priti's house as a valuable member of the welcoming committee, waiting for the prospective groom to arrive.

Deepak came over with a small army of relatives to meet Priti for the first time. Dressed in a crisp white shirt and beige trousers he looked pleasant but extremely nervous. It wasn't difficult to pick Deepak from the small army as he was the only young male in a group of semi-geriatrics. Priti was dressed in a red *salwar kameez* which had floral sequins speckled all over. A bit elaborate for daytime wear but she didn't have much choice as 'her' army thought she looked rather fetching in it. War paint was slapped on by her aunt that made her look at least five years older. Priti had promised herself that she would not be subjected to a public spectacle where she would meet her prospective husband and wait for approval nods from the audience. How can you marry a total stranger? He could be a complete moron! She had argued. But she was doing exactly that. In fact, marriage was never on the cards for Priti. She had seen too many staged marriages of her cousins to put her off for life. Many who had secretly confided in her about how unhappy and incompatible they were with their chosen spouses.

After both sets of troops had settled themselves for a round of tea and hot savouries, Deepak and Priti were cajoled into leaving the house to go for a walk just so they could 'get to know' each other. Priti and Deepak found themselves whooshed out of the house by an excessively eager relative. And I'd found myself down-graded swiftly from a respectful position of the bride's best friend to a glorified housemaid fetching hot beverages and more greasy savouries to a room full of merry Punjabis (who could seriously do without piling on more empty calories). Where was Neeraj? I'd looked around and spotted my subject of interest slouched alone at the far end of the lounge, looking vacant and unrecognisable sans his associates. He'd appeared pensive, probably pondering on how he was going to fill his days once Priti settled down.

Elsewhere Deepak and Priti had started walking towards a nearby coffee shop. Deepak made nervous small talk at first and then worked his way up to giving Priti a brief synopsis of his life. With his gentle, soft voice he brought her up to speed about his education in Mechanical Engineering and how he'd known all along that he would start his own business someday.

'Priti I am sure this must seem strange, you know with our parents orchestrating this little meeting but you can turn this proposal down if you don't like me. I won't take it personally. I have never dated or seen other girls. This might seem odd, as we've only just met, but I quite like you and would love to get to know you better,' he'd said.

He was 10 years her senior almost middle aged. What did she have in common with him? Priti couldn't help noticing Deepak's hands. They were clean and there was something about them. She has never known hands to have personalities. But these did. They looked kind and gentle. Her mind was made up. Firstly, she could not go through a similar ordeal - another walk with another stranger in the middle of the afternoon and talk about her life (or not, in her case). Heck! She would have to take her chances and say yes to Mr Kind Hands. So the hands did it for Priti. They were clean and kind. That was the mind of a confused eighteen year old for you. Nothing prepared Priti for what followed later. In her mind she thought a 'yes' would mean a long unofficial engagement while she completed her studies.

Priti's father made the sole decision of making her quit her studies as he planned to settle her down to marital bliss!

Priti had harboured secret plans of studying in the US, she had been preparing for her TOFEL and SAT exams not so long ago.

I was disappointed in Priti for not rebelling against her father's casual decision. As a friend, I could not see Priti look so helpless. She was getting weary fighting for her own rights and happiness against her family and society. What about her dreams and her ambitions? I even offered to stand up for her and make her father see some sense. He needed to know Priti wasn't ready to settle down just yet, instead she wished to spread her wings and experience life. But after having vivid visions of me dying a slow agonizing death at the hands of her father, she managed to coax me out of it.

A year later Diya, Veer, Sanjay and I found ourselves attending Priti's lavish wedding. 'Where's Rakesh?' Veer enquired with a glint in his eye, secretly glad that he hadn't turned up. Veer found him bloody hard work. They had nothing in common. Veer loved sharing his knowledge on acoustic music and enjoyed talking about himself even more which clearly fell short of keeping Rakesh engaged.

'Oh he can't make it tonight. He's busy prepping for his exams,' I said, feeling embarrassed with the lame excuse and somewhat responsible for his absence.

'Looking cool Nats, can see you have finally made an effort. What's with the sari? Is it all for my benefit?' Veer asked, tugging my sari. I wasn't quite prepared for the tug. I was concentrating hard on balancing myself on high heels which felt like walking on stilts at the time. I tripped and broke my fall by clutching on to Veer, nearly stepping on his shoes in the process.

'Whaaey…please stand well away from me; don't you go tripping over my shoes,' he said as he moved away from me. 'Check out these beauties, what do you think?' he gestured pointing at what looked like an ordinary pair of brown leather shoes to me.

'Hmm, they're alright, I guess,' I said gathering myself.

Veer looked devastated with my response. 'Alright? Alright?' he repeated the word gobsmacked, as if he was hearing the word for the first time in his life. 'You are just jealous!' he came up with a ridiculous conclusion. He was livid, his bulbous eyes raging with anger. 'These are G-U-C-C-I my ignorant friend. You need to get out more. I bet Rakesh's idea of designer shoes would be B-A-T-A (!)' he said, giving me spelling lessons on brand names again, making the others laugh with him. Veer had an unattractive trait of directing and hurling insults at people when his ego took a bashing. Particularly when it came to fashion, he thought he'd always got it 'spot on'.

'You are so unfunny Veer! Do try harder next time (!)' I said dryly, my words laced with sarcasm.

'What do you see in this guy anyway? He is a complete geek who has his head buried in books 24/7. Do you guys ever go out on dates? You were fun to hang out with and now you have turned into this stuck up little madam,' he said disgruntled.

'Veer, it is called growing up, something that you are utterly alien to,' I said, hoping to put an end to his annoyingly personal questions.

Just as I was plotting to accidentally step on Veer's new shoes to give him something else to worry about, we were summoned by Priti's parents to be a part of the reception committee when the groom arrives. We were probably the only guests who looked solemn in this huge theatrical affair. We all knew how much we were going to miss our special friend once all this was over. Like any other extravagant Punjabi wedding, this one was no different. Deepak, dressed in a cream and gold *sherwani* arrived on a white horse. Although it was hard to tell if it was him; he had a floral veil attached to his turban covering his face, traditionally worn by Punjabi grooms. He had a miniature version of himself riding with him, his nephew. One of the relatives held a huge red and gold embellished umbrella supported by a long red stick over him. This is traditionally carried over the groom to ward off evil spirits. The dehydrated horse looked like it could do without the fuss of having to wear an enormous fluffy red feather on its head and an elaborate red and gold cloth over it that completed its ensemble. The *baraatis* i.e. the groom's close friends and families who followed him on foot, tried desperately to catch the groove as they danced gingerly to jarring Bollywood music played inadequately by a live geriatric band. As close friends we joined Priti's family to welcome the groom and his *baraatis* with fresh rose petals.

I recognised Deepak's parents and his two sisters amongst the *baraatis*. We weren't the only ones to look solemn after all. For a happy occasion such as this, they smiled little. The two sisters were both married to rich businessmen. They had four children between them. They had a superior air about them, which strangely made me feel uneasy. I couldn't help thinking that they weren't a patch on our Priti. That was a shallow thought and was quickly ashamed of it. Priti looked stunning. Her designer bridal attire was specially ordered and flown from Delhi. Her aunt, the family's personal make-up artist was mercifully released from her temping duties and a professional was called in this time to work magic on Priti. Priti's otherwise cheerful mum looked visibly upset throughout the wedding ceremony. If my eyes weren't playing tricks, so did Neeraj. I urged Sanjay and Veer to have a word with him but both graciously declined citing personal issues. Priti's father broke down during the *bidaai* when the bride was being given away. That was the only time I'd ever wanted to give him a hug. Veer and Sanjay looked uncomfortable when Diya and I broke down on their shoulders. Veer looked more worried of the two, as my wet mascara had left stains on his new shirt.

Chapter Three

'Mum, how are we going to celebrate my birthday?' Can't wait to get my prezzies,' Rishab says, convulsing disturbingly with laughter at the mere thought. 'Don't be shy with your gifts Mumsie; any Playstation games or financial contributions into my piggy bank are welcome. I am going to be so rich!' Rishab shrieks at the prospect of turning 11 the following week.

'Well, you won't and there will be no parties! How do I gently burst your little bubble sweetheart...turning 11 is hardly momentous,' I say, crushing his plans of playing Mr Popular for the day.

'Oh, that's just tight!' Rishab's smile has been wiped clean. He looks cross, very cross.

'Well, call it what you like, but I can't be bothered entertaining your friends anymore. Old age is catching Rishab and I am not sure if I am up to chaperoning your dizzy friends for two solid hours! Last year was enough to last me a lifetime, it nearly killed me. In case you've forgotten let me jog your memory and remind you that I had twelve of your friends to supervise at the bowling alley, all high up to their eyeballs on fizzy drinks, sweets and cake,' I say making maniac eyes, still miffed with the little monsters who had created havoc running ragged in the super king-sized bowling alley. It'd left me completely shattered and undignified looking with bits of cake stuck in my hair as I rounded them up to hand them over to their respective parents who, with my luck, were unduly late to pick them up.

Rishab disappears into his head and gloomily considers options.

I can tell he has come up with several as he seems immediately energized with his thoughts. *Damn!*

'How about taking us out to the cinemas?' Rishab says, suggesting something safer for his ageing parent.

'Erm…no! Strapping and transporting half a dozen of you in my dinky car, sitting through another one of your mind numbing superhero films, taking you all in turns to the men's, fails to somehow generate a certain amount of enthusiasm,' I say as I rationally consider implications of the latest option.

'Just goes to show how much you love me mum,' he sighs. Rishab is a master at playing mind games.

'Err, don't you play the emotional card with me, kid. Why can't you ask your father?' I ask with utter annoyance at Rakesh's selective disappearing acts. Barring house parties Rakesh shows little interest in any other forms of entertainment.

'I am sure he'll be on call, he is always working on weekends,' Rishab retorts as he comes up with valid excuses for his father. I begin to wonder if he is his 'daddy's little boy' after all.

'Yeah and that's when I come into the picture. Good ol' reliable mum. Just because I don't work on weekends doesn't mean I don't work at all. I do have a job you know,' I shout louder as Rishab rolls his eyes like he has heard it all before. 'I have had a dreadful week and I just might want to put my feet up and unwind or even treat myself to a bit of retail therapy for a change,' I say looking at my shabby image reflecting on the French windows.

'Okay then, can we at least have my friends over? We've not had a party since ages!' Rishab moans.

'A party in the house? You say that so casually, it's almost frightening! What is it with you Rishab, planning an early exit from this world for your mum? Look at the bags under my eyes, can carry a week's shopping in them,' I say pointing at my imaginary pouches.

'Mum, puh-leash,' Rishab begs.

I thought slavery was eliminated years ago, but it clearly wasn't apparent in my house. That weekend I find myself hosting another one of my dinner parties in honour of Rishab turning 11.

Rakesh and I'd moved to San Jose, California, nearly twelve years ago. There is a fairly large Asian community where we live. We are all practically family now. So with a little help from Rishab we end up calling the entire neighbourhood. We usually leave our American friends out of the guest list when we have the Asian mob over and vice versa. I have suffered various forms of angina attacks in the past; planning a menu that's suitable for both the Asian and American taste buds. Rakesh, like his son, loves having people over, and why not? The house cleans itself and the food miraculously finds itself on the table.

I, for one hate entertaining. Although I should be a semi professional by now with the amount of parties we've hosted but nothing prepares me for these nerve wracking gatherings. I can't remember a time when we'd call less than six families over. It has forever been a mega event for Rakesh. He has never run out of names when we've made a guest list, if I did object, like Rishab, he'd call me 'tight'. I am not quite sure if it was the process of meticulously chalking out the menu by going through pages of hand written recipes handed down by my mother or churning out several dishes to keep up the reputation of being called a remarkable cook or making mindless conversations with the gang, that I detest the most. Whilst you are trying hard to contribute and listen to meaningless discussions, you are thinking about the dish that's baking in the oven, the starters that need warming, dishes that need staging and desserts that require assembling.

There are also the children who toddle in with the families. How do you monitor them discreetly without upsetting the over indulgent parents? There could be a creative one amidst them who might want to display his work of art on my magnolia walls or a poorly one who has had one too many meat kebabs and has now left evidence of it on my new taupe rug or Rishab's clone who'd rather save himself a trip to the sink and wipe his greasy hands on the upholstery. And then there are the over conscientious mums to cope with who would like to feed their kids 'on time' thus putting an end to my structural plans of scrupulously staging my food.

Rakesh is seldom home till food and the house is in order. And when he does decide to roll in just before the guests arrive, he'd be spending his time sprucing up, colouring his sparse fast disappearing hair, shaving his non-existent stubble, drenching himself with his favourite cologne (that is enough to give anyone who is four feet away, a chronic migraine), carefully picking his shirt for the evening and collecting his thoughts on how he's going to enthral his audience with his knowledge on current affairs and medicine.

'Rakesh, if you have done spending time with yourself, could you help me keep these in the fridge, please?' I say as I secure the cling film on two bowls of watermelon and feta cheese salad. I try to put Rakesh's services to use when I am really upset with him. Not that I couldn't put the bowls in the fridge myself, but it annoys me when he doesn't offer to help when I clearly need it. Rakesh's idea of help would be to choose appropriate music for the evening, although it still mystifies me why he takes as long as he does, as he eventually decides to play the same piece of music every time.

'By the way, I forgot to mention, I have invited Milind, he's that new junior doctor who's joined our team,' he says, ignoring my previous comments about him and taking the bowls from my hands. He loves having Indian junior doctors around him. He secretly adores being addressed as 'Sir' by them.

'Now, why doesn't that surprise me? I really wish you would tell me before inviting the entire continent. I have to make sure there is enough food to go around,' I say as I perform mental maths on head counts and food portions.

'Don't fret babes, we can always serve the food in smaller dishes so people make sure they eat less,' he says as he comes up with an instant solution.

The usage of the title 'babes' is usually profuse; especially when he fails to give me updates on the ever-growing guest list.

'Correct me if I am wrong, so we are inviting people for dinner so we can send them home hungry. Now look who's being 'tight'!' I say nearly bursting a blood vessel.

'Don't start an argument over nothing. I am sure you would have made enough,' he says as he puts one bowl on the top shelf of the fridge. He lifts the edge of the cling film of the other bowl and helps himself to four cubes of feta cheese.

'Oi! Stop that!' I slap his wrist with a wooden spatula. 'And with you around the food there will be none left to serve,' I say.

Having just enough time to slip into the first semi-formal attire I could get my hands on, I join Rakesh to welcome the stream of guests who trickle in bearing gifts for Rishab.

Unlike the frazzled hostess, the host performs his duties rather well. What has really begun to annoy me about Rakesh, is, his tendency to make folks believe that he has planned the whole event single-handedly. The usually sluggish husband miraculously undergoes metamorphosis and turns into an active and spirited host - pouring drinks and dishing out nibbles and bites, mixing cocktails effortlessly, playing the role of the family photographer, heating kebabs and bringing out the dishes giving an impression he has prepared them all by himself. I even catch him giving away an extensive recipe of Panna Cotta merely by guessing the ingredients. As he captivates his intense listeners (mostly women) with his carefully researched, scripted and rehearsed knowledge on new discoveries in medicine, I hear one of our female friends gush and whisper in my ears 'You are so lucky!'

As the evening draws to an end and we say our goodbyes to the last family at the door, the phone rings. It's Rakesh's mother alias 'Mother-in-law from hell!' She and her husband would be flying down to visit us in three weeks. Smashing (!) A perfect end to a perfect day. Is there a God?

Chapter Four

Rakesh comes from a simple middle-class Tamilian Brahmin family. Nicknamed - Tam Bams by the youth today. Tamilians, with the exception of Rakesh's mother, generally are a more intelligent breed. Tamilian Brahmins are from the 'priestly class', who inevitably gain immediate respect from other Tamilians in the community. Brahmins are firm vegetarians like my in-laws and so unlike my husband. I am guilty of being the first to introduce Rakesh to the delights of non-vegetarian cuisine and he has now progressed to someone who can eat anything that moves. Rakesh's father - Dr Raghu Iyer, a physician, by profession, had moved to Mumbai from Chennai, Tamil Nadu, nearly forty years ago, with his over bearing wife Maya. Most of the Indian Hindu names originate from Sanskrit language (the sacred and literary language of Hindus), and they have significant meanings attached to them. Maya means 'Illusion' in English. I wish our Maya had remained an illusion but unfortunately the harsh reality was that she was my mother-in-law, the Godzilla of Godzillas!

Maya disapproved of me since the time we'd first met. She had hoped someday she would have a simple stay-at-home daughter-in-law who would have no interest, opinions or desires of her own and her sole purpose for her existence would be to cook, look after and worship Maya and her family with utter devotion. Someone who would wear a nine-yard sari, humungous red dot on her forehead and appear painfully shy at all times.

As Rakesh had forgotten one of his assignments at home on that 'historic' day; gave mummy dearest a quick call, who in turn lost no time to beckon her chauffeur. As Maya emerged from a white, air-conditioned Fiat car, clutching on to a blue folder in our college campus, she saw a sight that would haunt her for years. She caught sight of a skinny girl with a short blunt bob, wearing a tight pair of torn faded blue jeans and a white tank top that read 'Guns N Roses' in fuchsia across her flat chest. She had a white and pink pair of Nike sneakers on and had one tiny pale pink pompom sewed on to the rim of each sock that reached up to her undernourished ankle. She wore a broad leather bracelet which had spiky silver studs embedded on them. This girl who clearly looked experienced in blowing mega sized pink bubbles with her chewing gum, had her skeletal fingers entwined with those of Rakesh, who was as it seemed, gazing at her with sheer fascination.

As Rakesh and I turned around, we looked at a heaving, circular, big breasted, sari-clad figure. Her dark, well-oiled hair was pulled back together to form a tight bun and a huge red hibiscus flower secured firmly onto it.

'*Ma*, that was quick! You are a life saver! I had spent the whole of last night preparing this. Oh and by the way, this is Natasha. Natasha, meet my mother,' Rakesh said as he lunged forward to grab the blue folder from the hyperventilating being.

'Hello Aunty!' I'd said keeping up with the Indian tradition of addressing anyone who looked more than ten years older than you - 'aunty' or 'uncle'.

The figure had now begun heaving even more as I smiled and chewed gum at the same time. She didn't smile back, it was like she was in a trance.

'*Ma*, are you alright? You look a bit pale,' Rakesh said as he looked genuinely concerned. I wondered if it had to do with the excessive amount of talcum powder that was liberally smeared on her dark skin. Most Indians from the south shared a mutual 'talcum powder fascination'. In their minds it served two purposes - a) it kept their skin dry from excessive humidity and b) made their dark complexion look lighter. In actual fact the powder infused with sweat to produce a grey chalky mask on their dark skin.

Rakesh and the grey masked round figure then stood away from me in a corner, ranting in Tamil - one of the oldest languages in the world. I tried to make sense of their strange verbal altercation by closely observing their body language (primarily consisting of animated gestures) and latching on to a few sprinkling of English words. The word 'love' was used many times over. It was pronounced differently by Maya – 'Lowe'. It was quite amusing to watch Maya's head shake robustly; dislodging her hibiscus flower from her bun and I watched it gently make it's way to the ground. The fact that we were an item became quite clear to the shell shocked Mrs Iyer. Maya was hurriedly bundled into the car after she suffered another attack of palpitations. Maya recovered swiftly from the sudden bout of breathlessness as she was ferried home. She possibly gulped copious amount of cold water to cool her raging body. She managed to pull herself together and then on focused her energies to visit every temple erected in the city of Mumbai, worshipping various idols, offering numerous garlands of flowers and coconuts, feverishly chanting holy hymns like she'd seen a ghost, praying for me to vaporize from this planet.

Maya would disconnect my calls to Rakesh unceremoniously which I thought was quite rude. Then she went to the next level - giving me threats in Tamil and the next level after that - mouthing threats in English, in case I was lost in translation. Who does that? This made me more determined than ever to be with Rakesh. Rakesh was far too enamoured by me to give in to his mum's ludicrous demands. He was smitten by me the minute he'd spotted me on our first day in college – our induction day. So did four of his other friends which he'd mentioned after we got to know each other, which I found quite flattering. He couldn't believe his luck when we became an item. He surely couldn't give me up just like that, especially when it took him months to muster up the courage to ask me out. Not to mention his four friends waiting by the wings for things to go sour between us. Rakesh's father being a well educated and fairly broad minded individual, remained neutral to the drama. He had much more important issues to attend to, like his dying patients in his little clinic, located in the fringes of the city.

Godzilla finally thought her prayers would be answered when Rakesh moved to Pune, situated just over 75 miles from

Mumbai, to study medicine. She thought the distance between us would finally help Rakesh come to his senses. I sometimes wondered what the attraction was. Was he worth all this grief? I did have pretty boys, like Rakesh's cronies acting funny around me. However, most of them fancied themselves more than they fancied me. They wore more jewellery than I did and had longer hair than mine. Rakesh was different in more ways than one. He used the public transport despite having access to a spare car at home. He had an answer to any difficult question. It was inspirational to watch him so driven and motivated about life unlike me who clearly lacked direction.

I am one of the two daughters to my glamorous Bengali parents - Mr Bijoy and Mrs Shoma Roy, who in complete contrast to Maya, were moderately progressive in their thinking. My older sister, Tina and I were raised in South Bombay, where the rich industrialists and elite reside. My father ran his own advertising and event management agency with my mother as the Creative Head in it. It did amaze me how my mother juggled her career and home with such expertise. I am sure it wasn't easy for her to work with my father as he would quite often lose his temper in a room full of professionals. It sadly came with the territory. The luxury and flexibility of working from home on many occasions was one of the perks that not many would offer at the time.

They met as students of Architecture in Kolkata. As they belonged to the same community, their parents didn't object to their courtship. After a brief stint in a building firm, father married my gorgeous mother and they soon relocated to the land of dreams - Mumbai. It was a bumpy ride at first, but having each other for support and a little financial aid from their families, it didn't take them long to show the world that they'd arrived.

Tina and I were spoilt rotten by our parents. However, there were certain boundaries and ground rules engraved by them which Tina and I couldn't dream of challenging. The boundaries and ground rules underwent periodic modifications as we grew older. As toddlers we were told to watch our P's and Q's. As teenagers we weren't allowed to smoke or drink but we were allowed to attend most parties, which invariably we chose not to, as we stuck out like sore thumbs. Being in the entertainment business, my parents had seen enough lives wasted on drugs and alcohol and tried to shield us from the ugliness as much as they could.

I, for one, was quite taken in by the glamour world. I often wondered why my parents would scout for new faces when they had one (two in fact) right under their nose. I decided to surprise them one day by raiding Tina's wardrobe and make up and invited our agency photographer home to work on my portfolio. Not surprisingly, it wasn't one of my brightest ideas as the efforts of the photographer and the photographer himself got binned! I remember being grounded for one month and my self-righteous sister bore an 'I-told-you-so' expression through my difficult period. I personally thought this was a classic case of double standards as it was alright to use other daughters as models and not your own. I kept my thoughts to myself fearing a lengthier extension to my existing sentence.

Tina was annoyingly different from me. She was better looking and more intelligent than me for a start. We have three years between us. She was father's 'little angle' who could/would do no wrong. I personally found her quite dull. Unlike me she lacked spirit. Boys didn't interest her but books did; which was a bit of a shame as there were some strikingly handsome boys who would have quite happily, jumped off a very tall building for her. She would rubbish my contributions towards meaningful conversations with the family around the dinner table. She hated sharing the room with me as much as I hated sharing it with her. We shared a double bed with one study desk on either side of the bed. I wanted mine painted candy pink while she chose 'elegant' ivory. I had posters of WHAM with George Michael and Andrew Ridgely with their weird hair-dos smiling at me, waiting for me to Go-Go with them, on the doors of my wardrobe; while Miss Toffee-nose found the whole idea of putting up posters so down market. I was only allowed to play music on my 'Walkman' (equivalent to the present day iPod) with headphones on, despite being in possession of a music system which was the envy of many, as big sister wouldn't have it any other way.

I didn't mind shopping at Fashion Street where dodgy street

hawkers illegally sold bad imitations of designer wear in their portable stalls, at rock bottom prices. Although the novelty of shopping there had worn off after I'd been bottom pinched by one of many lecherous hawkers. I did manage to recover quickly from the nasty violation and hit him with my pink handbag and was pleasantly surprised when I remembered swear words to hurl at him in Hindi. I recall coming home and standing under the shower for two hours. Ugh! It was no wonder Tina looked down at these lewd hawkers.

Tina would patiently wait for our parents to make their quarterly business trips abroad to bring back genuine designer clothes, shoes and handbags. She would carefully scan the pages of 'Seventeen' and 'Glamour' magazines and circle the items she desired and hand them over to mother to add them to her shopping list. We were like chalk and cheese.

Just as I was beginning to have doubts on Tina's sexuality she surprised me one day by talking about her 'crush'. Before I could do a double take and splash cold water on my face, she begged me for my assistance to act as a human smoke screen so she and her nouveau beau could have a night out together.

'So, who is this mystery man in question?' I was keen to savour every bit of detail that was about to be unravelled.

'Ricky Bhatia, the new model for the Urban Power campaign,' Tina said as she tried hard not to meet my gaze.

'Well, well, well, look how the mighty have fallen! If memory serves me right, I thought you said male models were narcissistic? So what makes this guy so special? I am intrigued. How did you meet him?' I asked, looking at her intently.

'Well, I had to hand in the copy writing work that *Pa* asked for and he introduced us as Ricky was in the office at the time. Ricky offered a lift home as he was driving in the same direction. We just got talking and he seems to be a fairly intelligent guy. Did you know he has done his MMS from JBIMS?' Tina said her voice almost squealing with excitement.

'Oh! So THAT qualifies him to date Princess Tina, does it? Tina, this man is a chick magnet. He has a huge female fan following who are waiting to devour him and all much prettier than you. Do you know what you are up against? This has disaster written all over it.' I said fearing the worst. I always felt very protective towards my socially challenged sister.

'It's one miserable date, you moron! I am not about to elope with the man, besides I need help with my entrance exams,' she said. Tina at the time was in her final year, studying towards a degree in Commerce and was preparing for the CET exams as she aspired to pursue her MBA in Finance.

'Splendid! I knew this was too good to be true! So you are going to be coached and not couched by this hunk!' I said feeling slightly deflated.

'Where did you learn to speak like this?' Tina said shell shocked without really wanting an answer.

Veer was immediately called upon for his valuable services for a worthy cause. Mr and Mrs Roy were given the idea that 'the sisters' were going out with mutual friends for a meal, which wasn't entirely untrue. At table one sat Tina and our very own Indian Paul Young aka Ricky Bhatia and at Table four sat the human smoke screen and Veer. When I first saw Ricky in flesh, I quite fancied him myself. Tina had Ricky and I had Veer. Needless to say, it was a very long night.

Chapter Five

'It is nice to see someone enjoying themselves (!)' I said looking irritably at Veer who had mastered the art of sticking two plastic straws up his nostrils without blowing them off whilst he exhaled.

'And you are a bundle of laughs (!) What are we meant to do here while your sister bats her eyelids at Mr Six Pack?' Veer asked reluctantly, pulling the straws from his nasal cavities and placing them dangerously close to my serviette. I helped myself to a fresh plastic straw from the silver straw rack on our table and skilfully flipped the contaminated straws to the ground, feeling considerably relieved with their disappearance.

'You have no idea about the gravity of the situation, do you? We are here on a vital mission to make sure Urban Power doesn't take advantage of my vulnerable sister. She isn't very experienced in handling strange men like you. Can we try to look a little less conspicuous and not attract further attention? I should have known better. I should have come with someone more reliable. Can we order something now? I am famished,' I said exasperated as I pulled the menu that lay beneath Veer's dark elbows. It was in similar situations that I missed Priti, who incidentally after having settled into a life of connubial bliss seemed to have forgotten the existence of her friends. After several one-sided attempts to stay in touch, I had accepted defeat and had grown closer to Veer.

'Why is everything such a drama with you? Why are you being so uptight? Chill and enjoy my scintillating company. Isn't that what you are really after? Admit it, you furtively fancy me.

All this palaver about chaperoning your big sister, who seems perfectly capable of looking after herself. Tell me this is just an excuse to ask me out. Don't you just love the women of today; they ask you out on a date and even pay their way through. So, what am I having tonight Nats?' Veer asked as he rolled his tongue over his dry lips and flashed his heavy eyebrows, a sight that was enough to make me rapidly lose my appetite.

'A black eye for a start!' I said, getting a bit weary of Oo-look-at-me-I-am-so- irresistible routine, especially when he couldn't be more further away from the truth.

I remember being slightly perturbed by his presence that night. I wasn't sure if he was outrageously flirting with me or just out to annoy me. I detested his nickname for me. We Indians do love re-christening people with odd-nicknames like one unusual name isn't tragic enough to live with. Veer had once hit upon the idea of calling me 'Nuts' which was swiftly changed to 'Nats' when he got rewarded with a bump on his head for originality. I was in denial about the unfortunate fact that we were tight buddies.

I remember my first meeting with Veer, it was our first day in college. Nothing prepares you for your first day in college. You spend hours dressing up in the most outlandish clothes hoping to make a huge impact on your fellow students, desperately trying to stand out of the crowd and get noticed instantaneously by every attractive individual of the opposite gender or the same gender as the case might me. I did manage to get noticed but not quite how I'd imagined.

I ambitiously attempted to wear Tina's blue mascara having no appropriate guidelines on its application. Although I had watched Tina apply it effortlessly on many occasions and to me it didn't appear to be rocket science. I went straight for the pupil and probably hit the retina. With minutes to spare and a punctured eye to deal with, I promptly abandoned the blue mascara and opted to go for the bare faced look. Not looking too pleased with the end results, I grudgingly made my way to college where an immaculately dressed Priti awaited me making me look like her red eyed underprivileged friend. It wasn't a good start.

Twenty thousand students were ushered into the college auditorium. Priti and I scurried along clinging on to each other and our respective folders containing blank A4-sized papers, terrified of being amidst innumerable unfamiliar faces. We've never questioned the objective behind going equipped with blank sheets of papers on induction days. But we do it year after year like it's a security blanket, a must-have. We scampered into the dimly lit auditorium and managed to find a few vacant seats at the back. Having nearly blinded myself in one eye, I chose a seat that had its leather covering slashed open and the foam protection scooped out. Criminal damage, probably committed by a former attendee who had let 'rip' his frustration of sitting through an unexciting dreary event. I only realised this when I sat my derriere down into this cavity. Before I could gather my body and pull myself out of this never ending pit, the lights went out and the seats next to mine were taken. Priti was completely unaware of my sorry state.

'Are you okay down there?' I heard a male voice whisper. I turned my deformed body and squinted to focus my vision on what looked like an average face bearing a very wide grin. Before I could even fake a dignified posture, I felt a force on my left arm that hauled me to a level where two folders could be thrust between the great big crater and my sore posterior.

'Thanks,' I said feeling rather sheepish. Couldn't have made a better impression, I'd thought at the time.

As the Principal of our college addressed and briefed us on how he was pleased to see a room full of bright, fresh and enthusiastic students who were the future of Indian economy, into a microphone that squeaked and echoed more than it should, I tried to maintain the equilibrium of the folders that defended my buttocks from the huge hole. Not surprising, the induction seemed unusually long drawn. As we finally got to see broad daylight again, the kind Samaritan introduced himself as Veer and Diya and Sanjay as his friends. Diya and Sanjay apart from the obvious difference in the anatomy in the upper region, strangely looked almost identical and seem to be enjoying their company far too much to be affected by the induction or at the prospect of making new friends.

Veer was even more average looking in daylight. He had worn a black T-Shirt teamed with a pair of black Levis Jeans. The T-shirt had 'Def Leppard' imprinted in old English font. A bit bleak for first-day-in-college wear but what was deeply worrying was that his clothes and his trainers looked spanking new. He had a coarse broad set of eyebrows but a feathery, wispy almost non-existent moustache. Almost like a few stray weak hair follicles had lost their way from the forehead and found themselves on the upper lip. He was the same height as me. I'd thought 5ft 6 inches would be stretching it. He carried a small beige linen haversack with no real contents in it and it hung almost limp on his left shoulder. There was deliberate usage of the words such as 'cool', 'wicked' and 'awesome'. Veer was a stereo typical 'wannabe'. The exact specie of homo-sapien male Tina and I would run from.

For a first date Ricky and Tina were doing remarkably well. They appeared to be extremely comfortable in each other's company. Ricky was oblivious to the fact that his date had got two additional sets of eyes along with her that night. And could you blame him? He could barely tear his eyes away from her. She looked astoundingly beautiful in a deep red chiffon dress with chandelier earrings. I observed Ricky look almost mesmerised by his elegant companion and I was mesmerised by him. While Tina had Ricky swooning over her, Veer had me forcibly engaged in a conversation about himself. There was no justice in this equation.

'Nats, could I ask you a deep question?' Veer asked, while he masticated his Chilli Chicken and took swigs of cold lager all at the same time, thus rudely interrupting my closer scrutiny of Ricky's devastatingly refined features.

'Only after you've swallowed the food in our mouth, I don't want remnants of it flying my way,' I said looking at a small particle of food hanging loosely from Veer's lower lip.

'Would you go out with me if you finish with Rakesh?' Veer asked casually with zero eye contact.

'And why would I do that?' I asked nonchalantly. Although my head was buzzing with questions, I failed to comprehend where this was stemming from.

'Because we could be good together?' Veer asked with a drawl, displeased with my harsh choice of words. Veer was more American than most Americans. A majority of his sentences were queries.

'I think you've had far too much to drink,' I pointed out in case he hadn't noticed.

'You spend more time with me than with him. We share an amazing chemistry. We are on the phone every night....I could go on...' Veer explained his drunken reasoning supported with factual points.

'Can we not have this conversation? We are just good friends... and that's it...end of!' I interrupted feeling uncomfortable with where the conversation was heading.

'You're right. I have had far too much to drink. Let's just forget we've had this conversation.' Veer said as his face changed colour. He appeared visibly hurt at being shot down to smithereens in seconds.

'Fine by me!'

That night changed four lives. Ricky and Tina discovered they were soul mates after having one Indo-Chinese meal together. After many clandestine meetings that subsequently followed later, Ricky proposed marriage to Tina. The Roys took a while to recuperate from the bolt out of the blue when Ricky paid them a visit one fine Sunday afternoon, which they thought was for a prestigious modelling contract but turned out to be their precious daughter's hand in marriage. Father was unhappy with the alliance initially as he didn't perceive male models to shoulder domestic responsibilities. But he eventually came around and gave his blessings to the love sick couple. What actually worked in Ricky's favour was that he came from a cultured and extremely affluent family.

Veer and I tried to deny the feelings we harboured for each other. It was uncomfortable at times to be around each other after that brief moment we shared at the restaurant. We tried to avoid crossing paths as much as we could. Although I was strangely flattered with his romantic outburst, I felt a loss of a good friend.

Veer had a distinctive dry sense of humour that at times was almost child-like. I enjoyed the friendship we shared, it was special. I had the exclusive authority to ridicule him without him getting a least bit affected (well, on most occasions). But it was hard to take him seriously when he would talk about his brief obsessions on pretty girls who had nothing going for them in the upper compartment.

On the personal front, Veer was silently enduring a difficult period as he struggled to come to terms with his parent's separation that year. And I was the only friend who knew this. I tried reaching out to him despite all the awkwardness that surrounded us, but it was too late. He had flown to Ohio to study Photography. Veer didn't think it was imperative to let me into his plans and flew out without saying goodbye.

Chapter Six

'Mum, are you alright? You haven't uttered a word since we left home,' Rishab asks, perplexed with his mum's sudden unusually rare transformation into a soundless and uncommunicative personality.

I was worried as well, worried if I was ever going to survive my four month sentence with the narky vegetarian brachiosaurus – Maya. Rishab and I were on our way to Mineta San Jose Airport to receive Maya and Raghu. There were very few occasions when I got Rakesh's explicit permission to drive his precious set of wheels. He was a proud owner of a metallic silver C class Mercedes-Benz. My humble diminutive car wasn't big enough to accommodate Maya. I drive with disturbing thoughts swimming in my head – Maya, giving me a slow and excruciatingly painful death with her verbal diarrhoea. It mostly consisted of Maya's worthless advice on how I need to be a more efficient wife and mother.

We park the car in the 'Long Stay' parking area, not quite sure how long it would take our Maya to roll out of the aircraft. Perhaps the cabin crew had declared a state of emergency and were engineering a novel way to liberate her Gluteus Maximus that might be wedged between the aircraft's ill-fated seats. We made our way to the arrival lounge with no real sense of urgency. Rishab adored his grandfather but didn't share the same special bond with Maya for reasons best known to him. As I stand reading the digital scrolling marquee for flight arrival information, Rishab yanks my incredibly pristine white camisole, much to my annoyance.

'Mum,' Rishab says, 'they're here!'

From a distance, I catch sight of Maya waddling towards the pair of us. Raghu patiently takes small steps to keep pace with his overweight wife. With advancing age and mounting calories, Maya suffers from every possible illness related to obesity. Raghu has clearly failed as a family physician. He waves and smiles at us. Maya tries not to catch my eye and smiles at Rishab. I am not sure if I like Maya more when she didn't smile. She wears a perpetual frown so when she smiles; she smiles with her infamous scowl which can be quite terrifying and can leave damaging effects on few.

Maya has chosen to wear a crimson red silk *Kanjivaram* sari, the kind worn by young South Indian brides. Unlike ordinary earth mortals Maya considers travelling to foreign land an occasion to wear her finest gear. Maya has a rare gift of draping an elegant attire such as the sari in the scruffiest manner. It's draped high up over her three tyre blubber to reveal her dark swollen ankles with numerous varicose veins that appear to be on standby, waiting to explode any minute. The string of Jasmine flowers that are fastened across her bun, look as jet lagged as Maya. She has slung her treasured black leather bag that was gifted by Raghu on their thirtieth wedding anniversary over her shoulder. Rakesh has sadly inherited Raghu's trait of buying the most unimaginative gifts for his wife.

The bag seems to have taken a shape of its own after enduring years of abuse being crammed between the weight of Maya's hefty arm and her even heftier body. We wait patiently for over twenty minutes as Maya takes her time to cover the 50 yard distance between us. I can't help but notice that my in-laws have decided to travel light on this occasion, as apart from a small handbag there is no other luggage in sight. This is out of the ordinary for the couple, as the concept of travelling light on her annual expedition is completely alien to Maya.

'Rishab! Natasha! Are we glad to see you!' Raghu's spirits of reuniting with his son's family seem to be dampened. Although he is glad to see us, he is unhappy with the unpreventable turn of events. Their bags – all four of them couldn't make it to their connecting flight. Why couldn't you lose our Maya, I moan quietly. I fake a welcoming smile which goes unreciprocated by Maya. Instead, as I stand attentively listening to Raghu enlighten me about the airline's promise to deliver their luggage in 48 hours; Maya eyeballs my clothes with blatant disgust and disapproval.

Maya didn't foresee what was to follow. As Maya's worldly possessions were thousands of miles away from her, we made a quick trip to Macy's to acquire a few essentials for the aged duo. Sorting Raghu wasn't a problem but how do we find the right gear for Maya? I offered to lend my saris but how would she wear them? Clearly my blouses would be too small for her. She could barely get two of her chunky fingers through the sleeves. Rishab managed to find a solution to all our problems. The very Maya who scorned the sight of western T-shirts had to unwillingly succumb to the inescapable situation.

The two days that followed were Maya's toughest days of her life and the funniest days of ours. She wore her XXXXL T-shirt with the lower edges tucked under her bra which strained at performing a miraculous onus of supporting her huge breasts. She draped my slinky chiffon georgette sari, revealing every curve that could have stayed mercifully concealed. There were stifled giggles and secret glances exchanged across rooms when Maya made her appearance. We kept Maya captive and under house arrest till the luggage arrived, shielding the Americans from a sight that could have resulted in many hazardous accidents.

Maya spots the airline van whiz into our driveway. Energized by this sighting she scowls and beams with sheer excitement at the prospect of being reunited with her lost personal effects. The luggage is delivered by a very hairy and heavily perspiring Hispanic who stinks to high heavens. He smiles to reveal a set of badly stained teeth which he is blessed with, after years of smoking. He lingers on like his revolting body odour to make meaningless conversations with Raghu just so he can examine this strange creature draped in a very large piece of cloth, wobbling and circling around the delivered luggage.

All four bags had a tailored covering made of cheap chequered fabric, to make them scratch resistant; this was Maya's way of waging war against the atrocities committed by callous baggage handlers. The baggage tags from their previous visits were still intact; Maya had deliberately kept them on as mementos. She fetches her keys from her formless black leather handbag and opens one of the bags with great urgency. I have never seen Maya function with such rapid body movements. I observe Maya's face floods with colour for the first time. It is still a shade of grey only a tad darker. She slaps her tubby hands against the leathery skin of her face and lets out a spine-chilling cry.

'Aiyeoooo Raamaa!!!' This is the only bit of Tamil most non-Tamilians understand. The literal translation is 'O Lord'; often chanted by troubled Tamilians if things go terribly wrong. It didn't sound good.

We obviously have an ominous situation and scamper towards Maya to investigate the reason behind her hassled condition. She is looking around the room as if she is unsure where she is, like nothing is making sense to her. We crane our heads into the opened suitcase to find contents of the two bottled jars of homemade Mango pickle have decanted onto Maya's treasured *Kanjivarams*. The situation is irreversible; the grim fact was clear for Maya that the saris and pickle could not be salvaged. Raghu places his hands comfortingly on Maya's heavy shoulders. Maya has never looked so vulnerable. Her body begins to vibrate and tremble. Huge beads of tears trickle down her cheeks washing away the chalky talcum powder leaving black streaks on her chubby face. She slaps her forehead, this time smearing her huge red dot and shakes her head like she has just witnessed someone dying. Rishab looks confused and amused.

'Maya, you have saris in the other bags. You are just being silly now!' Raghu says, making the situation far worse than it already was. 'Aiyeoooooooooooo!!!!!!' Maya cries even louder and this time she thumps her chest making her huge breasts sway in different directions. Raghu, like the rest of us, looks helpless. We leave Maya to continue lamenting on the recent demise of her silk *Kanjivarams*.

Meanwhile Rishab gets his annual dose of books and Indian sweets gifted kindly by his doting grandfather. Raghu thoughtfully presents me with books on spirituality. He probably knows I would need them to see me through the next four months. I am extremely fond of Raghu. I enjoy our deep conversations on Indian politics and discuss world issues during our brisk morning walks and over endless cups of tea thereafter. He is a liberal minded individual, who persistently encouraged me to be a working mother while his wife grunted disapprovingly.

Maya has come bearing gifts besides jars of the notorious mango pickle. But they were all for her beloved son. Rakesh has no idea how unappreciated and unaccepted she makes me feel. Raghu is sadly aware of his wife's ungenerous streak but remains powerless against her stubbornness.

'These *dosas* are excellent Natasha. You must give Maya the recipe,' Raghu says, savouring the hot crisp pancakes (made from fermented white lentils and rice batter) with a generous helping of fresh coriander and coconut chutney. It isn't easy for a Bengali to churn out authentic South Indian dishes and Raghu admires this skill in me.

For the next four months I had to get creative at dishing out vegetarian meals. Every annual visit from the pious Iyers meant fumigating the refrigerator to make it meat-free for the vegetarians and spending a small fortune on new pots and pans (lest the regular ones were used to cook eggs and animal meat in them). Rishab being a strict meat eater wasn't understandably keen on the arrangement.

'What do you mean, give her the recipe! What have you been eating for the past forty years?' Maya scowls.

'I don't know, you tell me. All I have been getting is a round piece of white rubber that can be gnawed all day and you still won't get anywhere with it,' Raghu enjoyed winding Maya up especially when he had an audience.

I try not to burst into uncontrollable fits of hysterical laughter and concentrate hard on packing lunch for Rakesh, Rishab and me; whilst Maya layers her pancakes till the plate can accommodate no more. I stick my head into the refrigerator. I realise the need to fly past the local Asian grocery store on my way back from work as I have just one solitary, shrivelled up, geriatric carrot to work with for the evening meal. I give a few inaudible uncomplimentary titles in Bengali to the dedicated medicine man, who seems to have forgotten his domestic chores with each passing year. I leave Maya with handwritten list of instructions on basic operations of the utilities. I would have got more reaction from a lamp post.

I make a dash to Rishab's school in frenzy. Rishab sits utilising all his voluntary muscles to shut his eyes tight. He clutches onto the leather seat and his seat belt; hoping and praying he makes it to school in one piece. I dodge other reckless women drivers on school runs who appear transfixed, probably drugged to their eyeballs on Prozac. Perhaps each one have a Maya of their own lurking in their homes.

I bring the car to a grinding halt on a 'No-Parking' zone near the school gates, attracting displeasing looks from other parents. Rishab leaps out, thankful to have survived the journey unscathed. We blow our ritual kisses and assure our love for each other. I don't wait to see Rishab melt away, like I usually do. I am going to be late for work and I realise this is going to be a regular pattern for the next four months of my life.

I reach the sheltered car park of my workplace. I twist and adjust the rear view mirror to accommodate my facial image. My eyes sting as they well up with tears. It is day four and Maya has already gotten under my skin. What hurts me more than her insensitive conduct is Rakesh's denial to the situation. Rakesh had promised to stand by me when he went against Maya's wishes to propose marriage to me. Had he forgotten the vows we had made to each other? Where was the man I married twelve years ago? I have begun to realise I am tragically turning into a Stepford wife, diligently sweeping away our marital issues under the rug. Rakesh is meant to love, cherish and honour me till I pop my clogs but instead his patients and Maya have taken my place.

I feel isolated, empty and terribly unloved and unappreciated. Right, this calls for a night in with myself! I make a structured mental plan to retreat into the attic, where I have created my own sanctuary. My little haven gets me through some truly grim days when I have a fall out with the husband. The haven is equipped with our discarded last Stereo, television set and

DVD player, an assortment of umpteen scented candles, a comfy divan with a secret storage area under the mattress (where I stock over-the-top and over-sentimental CDs and DVDs), a couple of wine bottles and a singular goblet. I am going to wear the scruffiest PJs (which wouldn't be a challenge to find in my dreadfully tired wardrobe), apply a sea weed mask to revitalise my under nourished skin, dishevel my already dishevelled bone dry hair, slip into my snug Eeyore slippers and watch 'Up Close and Personal'. It's time to review a few pointers from Michelle Pfeffier; on 'how to get your man to standby you' to fix the premature cracks in my marriage. I can see myself sticking the entire box of facial tissues up my nose and crying my eyes out. The very thought cheers me up, instantly.

I swipe my badge making the spotless glass doors slide open and give a customary nod to Paul, our organisation's ageing homosexual security guard. The lobby smelt of his girly signature cologne. 'Good Morning!' he greets with great cheer. Paul never fails to brighten up my mornings with his 'camp' greeting and a warm smile. I've quite often wondered if he tweezed his eyebrows and manicured his hands in his youth.

'Hello Gorgeous!' Steve and Bob say in unison as I enter the office. I work for the local radio station.

Steve and Bob are the two office clowns and my favourite colleagues. We are a threesome, the almost inseparable trio and the station's Assistant Client Service Managers.

Chapter Seven

'Morning Campers!' I murmur unenthusiastically. Even Steve and Bob's passionate approach to life was not going to help me soldier on through this extremely challenging phase in my life.

'Jeez, kidda, that was one swell greeting (!) Keep up with your high spirits and you are sure to impress Mr Ricci. Hope you haven't forgotten your 'hot' power lunch date with him this afternoon,' Bob says, making me want to have an instant breakdown.

Mr Dino Ricci, our new client, an Italian octogenarian, is the owner of a spanking new glitzy Italian restaurant. When he wasn't hyperventilating and bursting a blood vessel giving orders in Italian to his young and naïve underpaid American staff, he plays sugar daddy to a twenty-five year old buxom vacuous blonde, struggling Texan singer. Every encounter with Mr Ricci meant convincing him tactfully that Ms Candy Floss, with frightfully high pitched vocal cords, isn't going to record the jingle or jiggle her silicone filled assets for the restaurant's commercial.

'You are enjoying this aren't you? How do you sleep at night?' I ask Bob, who seems to derive immense pleasure in attacking me with his wise cracks on most Monday mornings.

'Very well thank you...as I always dream of you,' Bob replies with a wink, tilting his head as he clucks his tongue, all at the same time.

'Steve, will you be an absolute darling and charm Mr Ricci for me? I have tried everything in my power to persuade him to consider using a profession singer - my raw Indian accent, phoney American accent, spirited Indian gestures coupled with a hugely appealing smile, even sign language and all my earnest attempts have been rewarded with one constant mystified look. Before he gets weary and seriously considers using his Italian connections to shut me up for good, could you please do something!' I plead with enormous conviction.

'We'll probably need to send Bob this time…I am full of cold and not the brightest button in the box today,' Steve says, slurping his hot chicken broth from his treasured cup that has never been rinsed since the time I've known of its existence.

Steve's chiselled nose did look unusually red. The long denim clad legs were stretched lazily across his oak wooded desk, strewn with every office stationary required by a demanding employee. Steve's desk was renowned for its clutter. A recent addition to this mess - an empty instant chicken soup sachet, lays scrunched on one of the empty box files.

The 'pending' file tray holds a few unopened envelops and a stash of used ear buds with vividly visible brown grunge on the cotton ends of the plastic sticks. I try not to notice a piece of chewed gum with human hair, stuck firmly on the right corner of his desk. His computer monitor bears evidence of sheer neglect in the form of inches of dust fluff and greasy fingerprints. Steve's little dustbin with an oversized bin liner stands empty and forlorn under his desk. It amazes me, how Steve finds exactly what he is looking for amidst all this clutter. Steve sits with his shoulders slumped, holding his cup securely, close to his chest, looking as forlorn as his empty bin. What is it with men and their man-flu? They appear pale and defenceless, almost like they are dying of some tragic incurable disease.

'Hey, did I miss something here? Man…this is so not happening!' Bob says, looking cheated as he sits by an equally shambolic desk.

Bob looks irksomely young for his age. When I'd first met Bob, I thought he was barely a few years older than Rishab, I was hoodwinked by his taut, freckled complexion and ginger red hair. I was quick to assume he would have been a high achiever to have reached an Assistant Managerial level fairly quickly, I had even begun to address him with affectionate titles such as 'Sweetheart', 'Darling', 'Honey', etc., and wondered why he'd react queerly - batting his golden-brown lashes actively, making me feel rather uneasy. That was when Steve politely stepped in to alert me about Bob warming up to me in more ways than one. I was understandably horrified to learn he was just three years my junior.

I remember seeing Bob in a different light from there on. The affectionate titles were swiftly stripped away from Bob replacing them with more appropriate ones - 'Dopey', 'Loopy' and 'Bob the Slob' - a recent title that was earned after we unearthed the grisly truth that he showered just twice a week! This startling revelation was uncovered when I'd casually asked him the reason behind his eternal youthful looks. I had secretly put it down to a few nip and tucks and regular shots of Botox. Nothing prepared me for the shock horror of discovering my colleague, who I have to unfortunately work in close proximity with, strongly believes that staying away from water was the next best thing for your skin, as it washes away the all important natural body oils that help keep your skin young and supple. Urgh! I wished his confidential beauty secret had remained a mystery.

And then there is Steve, two years my junior, a searing handsome man. It wasn't the most enviable position in the organisation to be working with men with poor personal hygiene and who were younger and prettier than you, not to mention bags of talent between the two. Bob moonlights as a stand-up comedian.

Steve, for one, never fails to surprise me; there are absolutely no boundaries for this gifted yet humble individual. Coming from a family of musicians, Steve is a member of a Jazz band that performs sporadically in smoky night clubs and trendy restaurants. I never understood how he juggles two professions with such ease, despite a personal setback.

Five years ago, Steve was married to an extraordinarily beautiful community nurse - Debbie. Sadly, she was brutally molested and robbed by a gang of savage teenagers one night, as she stood waiting for Steve to pick her up from a secluded bus station. This tragic episode tore Debbie and Steve apart. Debbie blamed

Steve for not being there on time. While Debbie struggled with depression and anxiety, Steve battled with guilt and self loath which ultimately terminated their unstable marriage. Debbie tried counselling; she fought hard with her demons but eventually decided to put the ghastly incident behind her by moving to Georgia, where her parents lived.

Pleased that now Mr Ricci was Bob's responsibility, I settle myself behind my super clean desk. Well, any desk would look super clean next to Bob and Steve's desks. I squirt the desk with my homemade lemon and vinegar spray and wipe the dust-free desk using a fresh cleansing wipe with sheer pleasure. I find this exercise more therapeutic than Chamomile tea. I notice a little pale pink post-it stuck on the edge of my computer monitor with a message written in Bob's illegible hand-writing. It reads –

'URGENT – call your sister asap. You can catch her on her mobile.'

'Bob, when did my sister call?' I ask as I walk towards Bob holding the post-it note and spray bottle in my hand.

'Uh yeah...sorry I forgot about the message,' Bob scratches his scalp to retrieve further information from memory. 'Yeah, she called about half an hour ago. She tried reaching you on your mobile, but you had it switched off. I personally don't understand the concept of you carrying one when you have it turned off on most occasions. I am not sure if you don't like the idea of receiving calls or that you don't want to be seen in public carrying that prehistoric gadget,' Bob says flatly as he digs out one large piece of wax from his ear and flicks it only after a close examination.

Bob is right; I do carry a battered prehistoric gadget only because the nifty newer models frighten me. Upset with Bob's keen observation and truly disgusted with his ear wax scrutiny, I squirt my organic spray, aiming directly at his unwashed redhead thus deodorizing him for the day.

'Oi! Behave! That's health and safety, that! Remind me again, how old are?' Bob yells as he runs his short stubby pink fingers through his thick ginger hair, looking visibly refreshed by the zingy whiff and secretly enjoying the attention.

As I try to revive and resuscitate my batter dead phone, I wonder why Tina would want me to ring her back urgently. Tina is quite sensitive to the fact that I hate receiving messages of this nature. I have become the official uncrowned worrier in the family, especially after I'd moved thousands of miles away from her and our parents. The slightest bit of upheaval would set my susceptible heart palpitating with anxiety. The situation has worsened after father suffered a minor stroke two years ago which subsequently abruptly ended Mr and Mrs Roy's schmoozing days. The reins were hurriedly passed over to Ricky and Tina who seem to have done a sterling job after the recent take over.

Ricky and Tina married fifteen years ago and are blessed with two miniature Rickies - Neil aged 14 and Tanav aged 12. They are the spitting image of their father who now with a few sprinkling of dignified silver hair looks incredibly handsome. Ricky and I sadly never developed a relationship. I am too distracted by his face to make a sensible conversation and he looks visibly bored rigid to keep a conversation going. Apart from Tina in our lives, we have nothing in common. But I have enormous respect for the man, for he is an every inch of a devoted family man, doting and indulgent father and still insanely in love with his lovely wife.

I anxiously punch on Tina's saved number and wait patiently to hear Tina's voice.

'Natasha!' she says, there is a hint of sadness in her voice.

'Are you okay? Is everything alright? How are the Roys?' We frequently address our parents as 'The Roys', it amuses us, when we do.

'We are doing good. It's your college mate, Priti.'

'Priti?' It's been a while since the name has been mentioned. 'Well, what is it?' I ask as I can now distinctly hear the rhythmic pounding of my heart.

'Natasha…she has been hospitalised this morning.'

'Hospitalised? Why?' I explode.

'Her mum called earlier, she had been staying with her parents for a while. They found her unconscious…she'd taken an overdose,' Tina hurriedly explains.

Why would Priti want to end her life? Though she'd distanced herself from her friends, we did know she was happily married to a gentle and soft spoken Deepak and has a young daughter from the marriage. She seemed content with her little world and had no room for anyone else.

'Hello….hello…are you there?'

'Yeah, yeah I am alright. How is she? Have you been to see her?'

'No, unfortunately, we have been inundated with work. I was meaning to, though. We couldn't get much out of her mother. She seemed distraught…I just know that Priti is in a pretty bad way,'

'I need to see her. I'll try to fly down with Rishab. I'll let you know once our tickets are confirmed,' I say as I hang up.

'Is everything okay?' Steve and Bob ask in chorus, as they walk towards me. It is sometimes quite unsettling to find Steve and Bob sharing the same thoughts.

'No, my day just got worse!' I say as I hug the cold infested Steve and weep inconsolably thereby contributing generously to the existing pool of gelatinous mucus fluids soiling the woolly jumper. As Steve holds me close, unaware of the tragic fate of his jumper, Bob makes himself useful by briefly giving us a group hug.

Chapter Eight

'Hey, come on now Natasha, I am sure everything will be alright. You know how we hate to see you like this.' Steve says as he holds my arms and pushes me back gently to look into my Panda eyes. 'Would you like me to accompany you for a few days on this trip? I obviously won't stay the whole length of time you are there. I just want to make sure you're okay, you have been through a lot recently and I don't want you to think you're alone,' Steve says nobly as I move away from him.

Steve has been my rock since my life has spiralled out of control. Steve knows too well that my family back home have little knowledge about my loveless existence lest they get upset. We have spent many evenings in the comfort of our office where we'd offer free and informal counselling to each other over endless cups of latte.

He tries to conceal his discomfort as he feels the dampness that has stealthily permeated through his jumper. Steve's thoughts are easily read by all. He mentally debates if slipping out of his soiled jumper would offend me and hangs on it graciously for a few seconds and then soon slips out of it, exposing his white Hard Rock Café T-shirt with a damp patch in the centre. I wonder if Steve's 'man-flu' has affected his thinking process.

'That's very decent of you Steve, but how can we leave HIM in-charge?' I say pointing at Bob with my moist squishy paper tissue. Bob is prepping to meet Mr Ricci, moodily going through my paperwork that has been meticulously filed away, with his saliva dampened fingertips. He's still wearing his loose khaki shorts revealing the top bit of his Spiderman underpants. He shows no signs of changing into something more appropriate for a client meeting. It was strange how the secretions from my tear ducts and nasal passages have ceased with the very thought of having Bob run the show on his own.

'Gee, thanks for the vote of confidence (!) Loving the faith you have in me (!) You do know I am in the same room,' Bob says, looking visibly offended with my uncaring remark, now holding my pink Barbie file on 'Casa di Ricci' close to his chest. A pencil which has its bottom savagely chewed is tucked behind one of Bob's pink ears, awaiting more brutal ill treatment that was yet to come. The laces of his tatty trainers are deliberately undone with numerous knots in them. I have resisted the temptation on many occasions to untie these knots but the thought of catching something unpleasant kept me from doing it.

'Sorry, I didn't mean to hurt you, but it would be unfair to leave you on your own,' I say quickly making up for the rude undeserving comment. I hate myself for being so insensitive. How could I have been so thoughtless? Sometimes I just which I'd process my thoughts before speaking them out aloud.

'I'll be fine, honest, if Steve wants to accompany you for a few days,' he assures me with a gentle hug. Bob is the most forgiving person I've ever known. Besides, he has known me for too long to take any offence. When I tease him, it's always taken in good humour.

'Right folks, would love to stay and chat and have more insults hurled at me but duty beckons. Gotta go and meet the Godfather, see you in a bit,' Bob says, pulling his shorts only to have them fall back to his knees again. He rounds up his gear which he thinks are basic essentials for every important business meeting - his grey man bag that's usually carried across his chest, a mobile phone and an iPod. Ear phones are thrust into each of his pink ears and the iPod hastily concealed in the back pocket of his shorts which bring them even closer to the ground. The grey bag held some rather odd contents, a laptop that had more downloaded games and music than anything else, chocolate bars and chips (some 'real Bob food' to sustain himself in case he got ambushed in unforeseen calamities) and a miniscule mouth freshener in case he got lucky! Bob did multitask occasionally.

He waves us goodbye with one hand, uses his other to relieve that nasty persistent itch on his derriere and blows a huge pink bubble with his gum as he waddles off to meet his new Italian challenge. That was Bob. Unfazed about any challenge life threw at him, one redeeming quality, I deeply admired. Bob has a distinct peculiar walk, it almost has a character to it, and every second step he takes is a tiny hop.

'Maybe it is a bad idea, I just thought you might need a friend and I could do with a bit of a break, especially after what has happened...I am still struggling to come to terms with Debbie seeing another man, Natasha. She was the one for me...I can still smell her...jeez man. Never mind...it was silly of me to have even suggested it.' Steve says, looking far more upset than Bob did.

Great (!) Now the whole world dislikes me!! I have really excelled myself this time.

'Steve, snap out of it! I am sure she would want you to move on as well. Shit happens Stevie, whoops....pardon my French,' I quickly excuse myself. 'Us female species are very complicated, don't spend your prime years pondering over what you could have had. Pull yourself together, pack that little backpack and make that trip to the doctors for your multiple jabs...maybe you are right, a change of scene is just what you need. And I really could do with a friend. We'll probably need to work on some serious rescheduling and organising. And if we arrange for a temp to assist Bob with odd jobs, we should be pretty much sorted for a few weeks. But I don't want you to feel obligated to accompany me. Are you sure you'll survive the treacherous South East? You haven't gone beyond Miami never mind Mumbai... do you think the multiple vaccinations would suffice? I mean, we are talking about industrial sized mosquitoes that will have you for breakfast, food that would give you instant chronic indigestion by the mere sight of it, pollution that could have some adverse effects on your vital organs, sun - so strong that even a SPF 70 sunscreen wouldn't work, torrential rains resulting in floods combined with sewage water that would sweep you to a different city...how long have you got? I could go on all day. I shudder to think how your inexperienced, anti-body deficient American body is going to cope in all these conditions.'

'No, I don't feel obligated! Like I said the offer still stands if the Doc doesn't mind,' Steve says, now clearly feeling unsure about his random decision.

I am rudely reminded of the fact that I had to run my spontaneous travel plans through Rakesh and the demonic Maya (who would relish the thought of squashing them with utter delight) before taking a small crew on this journey. How would she react if she knew a male friend was going to keep me company all the way? Especially, one that's as good looking as this specimen! Now I had quickly begun to relish the idea of being the first to witness a rippling effect on a human body by sending shock waves through each tyre of blubber that had formed uniformly across the rotund figure.

'Well, if you are sure…leave it with me.' I say reassuringly having no clue how I was going to even approach the subject prudently and persuade the husband to leave him in an unfamiliar territory i.e. 'caring responsibilities'.

 Food was often a good place to begin with when I embarked on a conspiracy of this magnitude. That evening my exhausted body cooked all the desirable dishes the 'Iyers' could devour; thereby releasing some active Acetylcholine - the happy hormones which would ably aid in giving that all important nod to any unrealistic demand made by the scheming and devious cook.

'Rakesh, Tina called this morning,' I say, slipping into my black slinky satin night shirt that got revived intermittently when I was in need of Rakesh's excessive attention; which had become increasing challenging to gain over the years. A few top buttons were carefully and casually left undone. Attention to detail was crucial.

'Uh huh.' Rakesh says, as he ignores my seductive posture which was rehearsed a number of times in solitude a few moments ago. The lip plumping gloss that was generously smeared to achieve a natural pout didn't seem to help either. Instead, pages of the monthly medical journal were being scanned with unreserved passion. He'd settled himself comfortably against two plumped pillows on the bed. I wonder if I had overdone the just-out-of-bed-messy-curls look, as I glance briefly at my image on the wardrobe mirror. I inspect the beehive hairdo that would've put Amy Winehouse's (bless her soul) to shame. The perfume, which came highly recommended by the lady (who was possibly wearing every product she sold, on her face) behind the counter at Macy's, guaranteed to bring men on their knees, was now bringing me down on mine with a throbbing headache.

'Priti is in the hospital, she tried to end her life Rakesh, isn't that terrible?' I say as I am steadily beginning to lose the sexy siren plot. I notice a long strand of hair, standing proud, defying gravity, pleased to have got missed getting mowed down by the state-of-the-art epilator. I try to pluck it out discreetly with my fingers whilst keeping up with the dangerous act of seduction. The annoying hair remains firmly rooted, showing no real signs of giving up its sordid life just yet.

'It sounds serious…I need to see her. I don't want to have any regrets. You know how close we were. I am thinking of flying as soon as my leave gets authorized,' I say.

'Natasha, I know I might sound heartless but be reasonable… my parents have just arrived, how can you drop everything and leave? I thought you and mother were making some progress. I think she is beginning to warm up to you. Sorry honey, I don't think it's a good idea,' he says as he goes back to imbibing some more medical mumbo-jumbo; clearly finding it more enticing than his delectable wife.

I didn't know what or who pushed the wrong buttons. The fact that I was feeling fairly unattractive spilling through a night shirt that could have been a couple of sizes bigger, or the tummy trimmer that cost me an arm and a leg, wasn't performing its functions very well (instead it had sucked in the nasty little bulge that had found itself a snug little home and placed it elsewhere - beneath my bosoms thereby blessing me with an extra set), or that I had got a resounding NO despite my earnest efforts.

'Rakesh!' I screech. 'Here are a few home truths for you. You don't sound heartless…you ARE heartless!!! You and I both know that your mother hates me…'making progress' in dishing out more grief, more like! My friend is dying and you want me to hang around and build bridges with someone who is only too happy to burn them down. Besides, the process involves exchange of dialogues which clearly isn't apparent in this case. I have been pussyfooting around her for far too long. What have I gained from this relationship…nothing, zero, zilch, nil, nought!' the words spew out of mouth as I draw imaginary circles in the air.

'When was the last time we had a proper conversation? I am just another piece of furniture to you. You want me to stay, so I can look after you and your parents. So no Rakesh, I am not going to let you play the lord of the house and rubbish this idea. I am making this trip and taking Rishab with me and that's that! This pathetic magazine gets more attention than I do,' I say as I knock down the journal to the ground with one of Rakesh's propped pillows with one sweeping Jackie Chan move, cleverly leaving out the bit about my travelling associate. It was going swimming well, why ruin it?

Chapter Nine

'Are we okay?' Rakesh asks hesitatingly, cherry picking his words, making a desperate attempt to avoid an encore of last night's sudden emotional outburst. I look across the room to see him emerge from his shower after a prolonged habitual session of shaving, dental cleansing, facial exfoliation, olfactory hair removal and colonic irrigation. With the door left slightly ajar, I notice that the remorseful husband has remembered to leave the shower room bone dry as he would do after every marital fall out. He dabs his wet hair gently with a soft teal towel taking extreme care not to disturb the few hair follicles that remained nervously embedded in his head. A twin bath towel has been wrapped around the soft spherical belly.

A late night in my attic/sanctuary can at times lead to fatal consequences. On this occasion after knocking down the medical journal, I zoned into my nirvana, where I subsequently reached a tranquil state of inebriation and over looked the need to set the alarm clock. This is when good parenting skills come in good use. Rishab woke me up demanding his Coco pops. He wasn't very pleased as precious time was lost looking for me, time that could have been well spent playing a game on his Wii or watching the fascinating world of slugs on the Discovery Channel.

Following the rude 'awakening', I had hobbled into the nearest shower room I could find. A quick drench under the cold shower was probably not the best course of action for a pounding headache and bad hair day.

'What do you mean?' I say as I brush my wild tresses. I am in no mood for the ritual 'aftermath talk' particularly since each strand of my hair now had a life of its own. I am upset as I couldn't afford the luxury of washing out all the hair products I had in my possession that had been sprayed and coated on for last night's disastrous seduction action. A thought briefly crosses my mind if I could brave the big-teased-afro-80s hairstyle to work. But getting disturbing graphic and explicit mental images of the devilish American twosome – Steve and Bob, bursting into fits of irrepressible laughter whilst capturing candid pictures with their mobile phone cameras, saving them for dull office parties and uploading them as wallpapers and on 'You Tube' to share them globally, I swiftly discard the idea. Getting nowhere with my brush, which had now lost most of its soft bristles, I gather my coarse hair and secure it with a plastic brown hair clamp.

'Were you serious when you said you have no plans of coming back from India?' he asks tentatively, not quite sure whether he was still in the doghouse, making more hair-contact than eye-contact. I knew my new hairdo had finally managed to grab his attention, but this time however for all the wrong reasons.

'I don't have time for this, we'll talk when we get back from work.'

'Babes, I do love you. You should know that.' Now with his 'doghouse' situation confirmed, Rakesh is using his predictable 'babes' approach to squirm his way out of it.

''Love!' You wouldn't know the meaning of the word if it leapt up and bit your bum and chewed up the apron strings that still tie you to your mum!!!' I quietly mutter and amaze myself for coming up with an original limerick in a flash. I sling my handbag over my shoulder wildly intentionally hitting Rakesh's lower abdominal protrusion.

'Aaaow, careful honey…of course I love you,' he reflexly covers his crown jewels, 'Is this about my mother again? Why are you being so unreasonable? We have been through this a number of times. Where is all this coming from?'

'Its coming from all the undivided attention I have NOT been receiving!' I say feeling slightly generous and supplying some vital clues to the failing psychologist.

'How many times Natasha!!! After all these years, to me you are still the most gorgeous woman I have ever ever known, come here you daft woman…though it gets a bit tricky to find my real woman under that contraption. Your taste in lingerie has intrigued me over the years,' Rakesh says, pulling me close to his semi-dried, semi-clothed body.

A few beads of water glisten against his dark skin. He smells feminine. I could tell he had been using my expensive, luxuriously rich rose petal shower gel. The strong lingering sweet smell had overpowered his masculine after shave. I hate the double standards men have, raising their eyebrows at women who splurge excessively on cosmetic products, when they end up using most of it themselves! I remember the time I had invested wisely on some gold dust – a tiny pot of eye gel which guaranteed to rejuvenate my fatigued eyes, poof the puffiness and banish my dark circles in a jiffy. Unfortunately this wasn't to happen. Rakesh cruelly came amid this phenomenal transformation. He'd emptied the contents one morning, in one liberal application, mistaking it for a tester moisturiser – one of the promotional freebie products that are often given away by staff who are dressed to look like the product itself, in local superstores.

'At least 'the contraption' serves its purpose – it 'supports' me unlike my husband!! I feel ashamed spelling this out to you…I am lonely, depressed and very unhappy, Rakesh, in case you haven't noticed, it's all down to you! Isn't it ironic that a psychologist is unable to diagnose his wife's anguish? It's no good being a flipping sunflower left in a corner when there is no one to nurture or water it,' I could have come up with a better analogy, but I was seething and this was the best I could do at this point of time. 'Wake up and smell the 'filter' coffee Rakesh…we have drifted apart. Maybe you are right; you should have married someone with a medical background, who would have 'understood' your profession more. I am aware of the Hippocratic Oath to serve humanity and all that jazz…but what about the marriage vows we'd taken? And when was the last time you spent time with Rishab?'

Rakesh appears thoughtful, unsure if he's got the salient facts right in his head.

'Never mind...you have far more important things to get on with so let me not keep you from your diehard patients, who must be queuing up to lie on your couch and tell you all about their tragic lives...we wouldn't want to disappoint them now, would we?' I say struggling to fight back my tears. When did I turn so nasty? I couldn't blame the patients for my husband's utter lack of time management. How sad am I? But I can't help the way I feel.

'You need to slow down, sweetheart. I can't keep up with you. Why do you take everything that happens to you so seriously? Surely my dedication to my work isn't a reason to split up, or is it?'

'You know what your problem is?'

'Why do I get the feeling that you are going to tell me anyway?' Rakesh knows the drill.

'You have never listened to a word I say!' I explicate as I push Rakesh to leave the room.

It didn't seem right, walking out on a fragrant and perplexed Rakesh. But I had been in the same situation for too long. I shouldn't have to beg for his attention, not like this. I cry, we make up, he goes back into his medical bubble, with his scowling mum not far behind and ignores me yet again. Rakesh was wonderful at making magnanimous promises, it was the execution that he had a problem with.

'Don't leave like this...' he begs.

As I shut the door, a small figure creeps up behind me.

'Aaaargghhh!!' I yelp.

'AAAaarrrrrgggggghhhhh!!!!', the figure yelps even louder. It's Rishab giving me another coronary. 'MUM!' he bellows angrily at me.

'What???' I wonder if he'd seen me polish two iced donuts earlier. *Nothing gets past this boy these days.* 'I should be the one upset for creeping up on me like this,' shouting and digressing the topic usually works in such situations. 'Now get a move on if you've finished your breakfast, we'll be late again! And no clever remarks about my hair!'

'I am not leaving until you tell me what you've done with Melvin,' Rishab looks like he means business with his hands folded across his chest and his little fingers drumming over his elbow.

'Melvin…who…oh you mean that ugly gremlin?'

'MUM!' he doesn't appreciate the name calling.

The gremlin alias Melvin was the wartiest, slimiest and the most hideous looking toad one could ever imagine. If nature had ever got something so completely wrong with its creations, then this was it. As my luck would have it, on one historic day it leapt into Rishab's hands out of nowhere. Giddy with excitement, the frog/toad was hurriedly christened and taken hostage in my watering can by Rishab and his mates. I silently watched in passionate horror as Rishab poured his affections on this squalid creature. He had technically obeyed all the house rules. "No pe(s)ts in the house". But being unable to venture into my own back garden for the fear of being attacked by the watering can infested amphibian, I began to plot an early exit for the unwelcome garden guest.

After several failed attempts I tipped the watering can ever so slightly with the help of a few slate tiles thrown from the safety of my kitchen window. As the gremlin hopped its way out of captivity, I mimicked its four legged leap on the kitchen floor oblivious to the knowledge that Maya who had tottered into the kitchen to satisfy her insatiable appetite, had stood behind me watching me perform my victory toad boogie.

'I resent the accusing look, what do you take me for?' I say, concealing my guilt with clever words and an Oscar winning facial expression.

'But the watering can has been tipped over!' he says, doubting his sleuthing skills.

'It must have been the gusty winds we had last night,' I lie, knowing I am being slightly economical with the truth.

'Gusty winds?' Rishab turns into a human lie detector and makes severe eye contact to crack me under pressure.

'Yes, gusty winds,' I nod confidently. 'I don't have time to explain...less jib and more action chubby Sherlock....roll into the car...NOW!'

'Or was it your hair that frightened him away?' I fail to find any humour with his inaccurate conclusion. Rishab giggles as he opens the car door, moving on with his life and getting over the loss of 'Warty' surprisingly quickly.

I book our air tickets the following week. There were very few words exchanged in the Iyer household. It was apparent maybe space was what Rakesh and I needed, although we did have plenty of it living under the same roof. Raghu appeared to have an inkling that there was an issue but said nothing. Most failing Asian marriages are sadly dealt inappropriately – bury your head under the sand and wait for the problem to resolve itself. The problems are seldom addressed.

The stigma of marital problems, separation and divorce still exists in the seemingly changing society. Our deep rooted culture and conservative society fail to equip us to accept and tackle these situations however permissive we may think ourselves to be.

Rakesh and I have unknowingly grown apart during the twelve years we have been together as a married couple.

The in-laws are summoned and the news of my sudden departure is broken gently. I apologize for the bad timing of my unplanned trip as my friend needed me. Raghu smiles and gives me a God-bless-you-my-child head stroke as though he is doing it for the last time. Maya gives out a sour I-hope-I-don't-see-you-again grunt.

'Listen, I want you to call me as soon as you reach Mumbai. Even if it means waking me up at 2 in the morning. Promise me that you'll give 'us' another chance...wait a minute...is that Steve?' Rakesh says as he wheels our luggage towards the check-in counter at the airport.

My heart sinks and my stomach contracts as I look at a familiar figure with long unkempt hair, smiling and waving his hands in the air at us. My carefully edited version of my travel plans is beginning to unfold as we walk towards Steve.

Steve, however, has no knowledge that I would have kept this piece of information about him being my travel companion from Rakesh. He has worn a white wrinkled muslin shirt with multiple ॐ printed in saffron colour dispersed evenly. The spiritual shirt is teamed with a pair of crushed white linen trousers, a string of small wooden beads are strung awkwardly around his neck. He looks almost radiant in the saintly attire. Steve could wear a sack and make it look like designer wear from Milan. Steve's plans are clear judging by his appearance. Steve has begun his spiritual journey and appears keenly geared for a life changing experience even before setting foot into the plane.

Chapter Ten

'Hey Steve! Howzzit goin', buddy?' Rakesh asks as his Americanised greeting loses its fizz. Since the time we'd moved to America and as we've grown older, Rakesh has developed a few traits that make me cringe – Pseudo-Americanisation being the front runner.

'Good to see you again, Doc! Thank you for letting your lovely wife lug me along. You have my assurance that she will be well looked after,' Steve smiles and gives the husband a macho handshake. He then zeroes his attention on Rishab. 'How are you, big fella?' he asks Rishab as he ruffles his hair.

Rishab smiles shyly but appears slightly unhappy to have his well engineered gelled hair tousled. He immediately attempts to pull and sculpt his hair to make them stand on end again.

'Err...if you could excuse us for a minute, can I have a quick word with my 'lovely' wife in private? I am sure Rishab wouldn't mind keeping you company,' Rakesh says, offering Rishab's reliable services and swishes me away leaving the luggage trolley with the two to watch over.

I anticipate a public crucifixion as I am being indignantly led to a corner. I spot an anxious couple rifling through their bags, possibly looking for their lost passports. Somehow their problem pales in comparison to my prospective gruelling interrogation.

'What's going on here? Why didn't you tell me Steve was joining you on this trip? Have you any idea what this might do to my conservative parents if they were to get a wind of this? Are you having an affair with Steve? Is this what the talk of separation was about?' Rakesh quizzes me with multiple questions.

'I knew I would get this reaction from you, which is why I kept it quiet. And no, I am NOT having an affair with Steve! I thought you knew me better than that. You know Steve has suffered a personal setback. He just wants a break from what's happened between him and Debbie. Besides he is returning back in three weeks whereas I MAY NOT come back at all!! Hope that has answered all your questions, now if you don't mind I have a flight to catch,' I say as I watch Steve getting acquainted with Rishab's Ninendo DS. Rishab has finally got his hair standing exactly where he wants it without the assistance of a mirror; he wipes the excess hair gel on his navy blue Capri to my dismay.

'I can't say that I am not disappointed in you. I am not happy about Steve flying with you. I thought you were going to see a dying friend. Doesn't look like it to me from where I am standing. I don't see how Steve fits into all this. You can't be serious about not coming back. I can't just let you and Rishab walk away from me. That's' it! You are not boarding that plane!' Rakesh proclaims as his frown lines become more accentuated.

'Please keep your voice down. You can't stop me. Maybe this is your wake-up call. I can see that I've finally got through to you. We both want different things from life and we are only making each other more miserable in the process and that's not doing Rishab any good. I am glad that you have acknowledged that there is a problem and that's a start. Give me some time to clear my mind. Maybe you could join us in a few days and we could talk then? I am still married to you, aren't I? I can assure you that there is no one else in my life. I can accuse you of a lot of things but infidelity isn't one of them, so I wouldn't do that to you. Look after yourself and will speak soon,' I say and walk towards the newly bonded pair.

Rakesh follows me quietly and walks towards Rishab to give him a hug, he leans down and whispers into his ears 'Be good and take care of your mum for me, champ.' Rishab nods his head soldierly while his spiky hair remains motionless. Rakesh fights the urge to kiss him on his cheek, but decides against it remembering one of Rishab's laid rules – kissing him in public was strictly not permitted. And I sense a sudden surge of affection towards Rakesh as I see him wave goodbye and walk away with slumped shoulders.

'I gather the Doc didn't expect to see me fly away with his family,' Steve says as we join a crawling queue to the check-in counter.

I watch an Indian man struggling to keep his large family and luggage together. About a dozen dilapidated multicoloured suitcases are piled one on top of the other on a single aching luggage trolley, possibly breaking a world record of some kind. The father wheels the unsteady trolley which seems to have lost its drive and refuses to play ball. He perseveres unaided clasping the family passports beneath one of his sweaty armpits. The wife rocks her wailing infant to sleep while she ushers the rest of the brood to follow their father. Meanwhile one of the sons has lost a fight with his older brother over a bag of sweets. Unable to accept his defeat gracefully, he sticks a big piece of gum on the unsuspecting sibling's hair. Their little sister who should be strapped onto a stroller is pushing a little pink stroller of her own with a weathered bald doll in it. She realises that there are far more interesting places to explore and heads the opposite direction till a smack on her bottoms makes her see sense.

'Sorry Steve, didn't mean to put you in an uncomfortable position. It's complicated. Anyway how did you organize your sacred attire? It's clearly not yours!' I say as I yank at one of his sleeves that are measured to fit someone three sizes smaller.

'You like?' Steve asks. I am not sure if I am meant to give an appreciating nod at this point, I decide not to. 'Well, there is this friend of mine who had been to Goa not so long ago,' I realise Steve wasn't looking for my approval, 'I bumped it off him. Just an idea to blend in with the crowd, I didn't want to look touristy wearing something else,' Steve says, pleased with his choice of key pieces he had put together.

'Contrary to what the world thinks of us, we are not just a land of curries, snake charmers and yogis. Some of the world's leading industrialists are Indians. We have one of fastest growing economies and people are more western than the westerners themselves. I am afraid you couldn't look more 'touristy' if you tried. But full marks for effort!'

'You are kidding me! Oh well we'll just have to see won't we? Anyway this is where I leave you briefly, sorry I have to make my way to the First Class check-in counter. I didn't know the doctor's family would be travelling economy…tut tut' he teases as we reach the end of the economy queue.

We join Steve a few minutes later at the departure lounge where we see him sprawled across three seats facing a glass wall. He sees us approaching him and sits up. I seat myself next to Steve. I hesitate briefly to put my handbag on the floor next to Steve's little rucksack but fearing the floor to be alive with the unknown, I play safe and place it on my knees. Rishab prefers to watch an airplane that has landed on the long luminescent runway.

'You look distant.....you okay?' Steve asks as he examines my face.

'Yeah I'm fine,' I fake a smile.

'So come on then, spill. What's with the complicated story?' Steve has a glint in his eyes. He gently hits my shoulder with his. I don't expect the nudge and lose my balanced elegant posture and stop myself from falling across the vacant seat next to me.

I try to regain my poise quickly and say, 'Where do I begin? You know ours was a love marriage, right?' I begin an earnest overview on the subject.

Steve chuckles 'What is a 'love marriage'?'

'Shut up and listen…back home there are two kinds of marriages… 'love' and 'arranged'…a 'love marriage' is when two individuals fall in love and get married with or without their parents approval and an 'arranged marriage' is when conservative parents zoom in on a desired groom or bride for their offspring preferably from the same community and higher social status. The concept of 'dating' is frowned upon by the more traditional families and if you have been a bit naughty and have indulged in pre-marital sex, be prepared to be ostracized. Fortunately for me, I have open-minded parents and was 'permitted' to find a groom of my choice which is why I fall into the 'love marriage' category.' Steve fails to look enlightened and suppresses a smile.

I continue, 'Sometimes I wish my sensible parents had chosen someone for me, seeing that I haven't done a very good job at finding someone compatible. I feel so disconnected from him. Rakesh is a lovely man but I think we are just so wrong for each other. When I married him, I thought we'd grow old together enjoying each other...just enjoying being married. I want some romance, drama, passion, spontaneity, injected intermittently... some indication that makes me feel alive. Rakesh thinks I can get all this by watching The Bold and the Beautiful! I just wish I had a crystal ball back then and foreseen what the future held for me, maybe then I would have been with someone who shared the same energy and vibe. Someone who would pleasantly surprise me everyday,' I say as I ponder over my unrealistic thoughts.

'You are not alone. Everyone has problems, some bigger than others but that is what makes life challenging. We learn, we adapt, we grow and that is how we get on with life. Look, I am no expert, but if you are truly unhappy then I think you need to do what's best for Rishab and you. You have just one life Tash, don't let anything get in the way of your happiness,' Steve says, looking sagely.

'My word Steve! Where did all those nuggets of wisdom come from? This religious gear has certainly given you divine and supernatural powers,' I tease him. Steve shakes his head and looks mildly annoyed and embarrassed.

Travelling with Rishab has its advantages and we get to board the flight with First and Business Class passengers as parents travelling with young children get preferential treatment. Rishab is none too happy to be classified as a 'child' and refuses to jump the queue. I enlarge my eyes (an effective trick I learnt from many Indian parents) at Rishab without Steve's knowledge and Rishab reluctantly changes his mind.

Steve and Rishab swap seats as Steve wants Rishab to experience the high life flying First Class. A pretty flight attendant whisks Rishab to find his seat while Steve and I trudge along behind other fellow economy travellers. Some find their seats before us and prefer to leave us standing till they triumph in squeezing and shoving their hand luggage with incorrect dimensions into the cabin bag compartment. We finally find our seats at the tail end of the aircraft. We are fortunate and relieved to find that the aisle seat next to ours isn't claimed. Steve spreads himself across two seats and pledges he wouldn't disrepute the pious threads and steers clear of alcohol but instead voices his desire to spend his time sober learning the colloquial lingo with a little help from me.

I first check up on Rishab squeezing past passengers who are already queuing up to use the in-flight toilets. A sour, pungent odour fills the air as a passenger emerges from the facility looking visibly relieved. Ugh! No drinking fluids I remind myself.

After 'this is awesome mum!' verdict, I quickly retreat to my seat to commence my language class. But not before reaching out to a wet wipe provided by the airlines. I clean the arm rests on either sides of my seat and then turn my attention on the collapsible food tray. I fold the used wipe into a tiny rectangle. I open the little flap on one of the arm rests and dispose the wipe using my finger tips while Steve watches me with amusement.

'You know your biggest disadvantage is your skin colour…a dead give away. Be warned the street beggars will gravitate towards you as soon as they set eyes on you!' I caution Steve with maniac eyes.

'You're joking! How do I handle this scenario?' Steve panics and takes a gulp of his aerated drink from a little plastic cup and munches on some salted macadamian nuts.

'Fear not…just say - *Main…phirang…hu…..Mujhse… poorah… paisa…lo.*' I break the sentence into singular words for the new pupil and hold back a smile.

'*Mai…firaang…you. Moosi…pyuraa…paysa…loo.*' Steve repeats the carefully memorised words but not before putting a twist on it with his American twang 'What does it mean?' he asks curiously.

I nearly kill myself laughing but I don't have the heart to tell the eager learner that I've just taught him to say, 'I am a foreigner. Please take all my money!'

'You are such a tease! Something tells me you are not to be trusted, missus. I am sticking to English, thank you very much (!)'

Chapter Eleven

It is nearly two o'clock in the morning at our final destination and the aircraft is minutes away from hitting the Indian soil. It is over a day since we'd set off. Steve is lying comatose next to me, blissfully unaware that he has kept me awake with his synchronised high decibel snoring through his chiselled nose and low decibel whistling through his slightly puckered mouth. The suave image I had of Steve is shattered as his snoring hits a higher note.

I have admired and envied travellers who could sleep through their journeys. I, on the other hand, feel rough. I reach for my handbag that has been tucked away on an airline magazine under my seat. I rummage through it to find a miniscule travel mirror that has a clever inbuilt light. The mirror is usually placed in the inside pocket and I find it in its home. I praise myself for being so organised. But I almost shriek when I see a ghastly image on the mirror staring back at me. I haven't slept through the journey and it shows. A million blood capillaries have formed a red mesh around my eyeballs. My moisture-less skin bears a dull ashen colour due to lack of fluids in my arid and dehydrated body. The 'kiss-proof super stay' caramel delight lipstick has run out of steam but proclaims it hasn't entirely failed in its efforts as there is still some colour around the edges of my mouth.

I couldn't possibly let Steve see me like this. As most of the lights in the aircraft have been turned off, I attempt to do a blind search as I stick my hand into my bag yet again and use it as a radar to hunt down the absconding lipstick. I pick and feel numerous items in the bag that come close to the size and dimensions of it. I am surprised to find a large number of objects that match the description of my lipstick – nasal inhaler, mini travel toothbrush, lip balm and then finally find the one thing I am after. I use my left index finger as a barometer to gauge the depth of Steve's state of unconsciousness by prodding it into his firm abdomen. It didn't feel the same when I performed a similar test on Rakesh's soft belly. I improvise the abdominal prodding by using my entire hand this time. Even in less than flattering position Steve's body looks almost close to perfection. I am quickly ashamed to find that I quite enjoyed the prodding and briefly question my integrity. It has barely been a few hours since I have been away from my husband and I find myself attracted to my close friend. I hold Rakesh responsible for planting seeds of infidelity in me. I take a deep breath and resist the temptation to execute another pleasurable prod test and focus my energies on an unattainable mission. I turn on the overhead light. I then position the tiny mirror to accommodate my face and begin my earnest attempts to redefine and reorganise my lost features.

Just as I am about to take on the mammoth challenge I can sense some movement next to me. The snoring and the whistling seems to have died down. I quickly turn my back against the moving figure and find myself facing the little oval glass aircraft window. I curl up and bring my knees close to my chest thereby giving an appearance that I could be asleep. I am pleased and even reward myself with a few brownie points for quick thinking. I try to remain still and hold the mirror and the lipstick close to my face. With one swift move I smear caramel delight on my pale mouth. At this stage I am not quite sure why I am holding the mirror against my face since my mouth is too magnified to see where it begins and ends.

'Err…what are you doing?' I hear Steve's groggy voice behind me. I look at the reflection on the glass window. I can see my contorted body holding the mirror and caramel delight while Steve has now leaned forward to look into my hollow eyes on the glass reflection. I am too embarrassed to face Steve. I remain frozen like a stunned animal in front of glaring headlights. The brownie points soon turn to colossal zeroes.

I take my time to turn around and realise that the amateur contortionist might require wheel chair assistance for the rest of her life.

'Jesus Christ Tash, who beat you up? Is this what you look like when you get out of bed?' Steve laughs too loudly for a man who has just woken up from coma. I seriously contemplate on shoving the nasal inhaler, travel toothbrush, lip balm, caramel delight and the mirror in quick succession, up Steve's nose. His body now looks less than perfect.

'I'll beat you up in a minute if you don't shut it, how can you laugh at me like that, especially when I have silently and painfully endured sleep deprivation caused by your consistent thunderous snoring,' I say, pointing at exhibit A – my bloodshot eyes.

Just then a bilingual flight attendant makes an announcement to fasten our seatbelts and remain seated as the aircraft is about to descend. I am pleased with the welcome intrusion into my mortifying moment with Steve, who still bears an annoying grin. I whack him with my handbag after throwing in the mirror and lipstick, in a vain attempt to wipe off the smug grin before tucking it away; he winces unapologetically with a broader grin.

Steve and I are not quite sure if the announcement about fastening our seatbelts is assimilated amongst the Indian passengers as most of them have now sprung up from their respective seats and are dangerously close to causing some serious accidents by opening the overhead compartments to haul out their compressed hand luggage. The seatbelt fastened obedient passengers bear worried looks and apprehensively brace themselves for a luggage avalanche. An Indian male attendant repeatedly urges them to return to their seats in Hindi, but the passengers prefer to ignore him and continue their quest. The victorious passengers remain standing with their retrieved belongings. I resist the desire to politely intervene to say this approach isn't going to help them reach their destination any quicker. I squirm as my country folk let me down with their unwise attitude. Steve looks amused yet again. I get the feeling I am going to see a lot more of this expression as he unearths our inimitable idiosyncrasies in his travels around our exotic land. The immovable passengers are thrown back into their seats by the force of the shuddering aircraft when it speeds over numerous crevices and bumps on the airstrip. The folly passengers exchange defeated looks.

As we say our goodbyes to the crew who look only too happy to see the last of us, we spot Rishab with two identical flight attendants near the exit door. His possessions seemed to have multiplied in the form of various First Class souvenirs. He looks worn out and shabby like his mother. He yawns and stretches himself to establish his fatigue. His vertical spiky hair, having weathered harsh conditions of Transatlantic travelling, is now standing at every other angle except the desired 90 degrees. The Mumbai humidity hits my hair and it soon frizzes up into a fuzz ball. We have no time to exchange pleasantries or notes on our bad hair day issues after our reunion. Steve and I drag him with us like our excess luggage as we dart towards immigration. A young Indian woman in her twenties decides her need to reach the immigration counter is greater than ours and whizzes past us, wheeling her cabin bag over my feet. I am too tired to protest and let her get away with GBH. Steve looks surprised at my forgiving attitude.

We walk miles on an endless passageway. The airport has been refurbished but through the eyes of a new visitor it looks neglected. The carpet appears dusty and worn out. There are a few soulless potted plants dotted around on either sides of the passageway that are screaming for attention. The bins have been used as spittoons by *Paan* (tobacco and spices filled in beetle leaves) eating staff and police constables. A cleaner leisurely strolls past an overflowing bin with an empty bin bag and a pair of rubbish picking tongs. He displays the dual purpose of his tongs as he waves them in the air, with a chocolate wrapper stuck to it, to greet the newly arrived jet lagged passengers. Rishab politely waves and yawns at him as he is being lugged away by his limping mother.

The weary mother-son duo use the escalator to reach immigration while our well rested Steve prefers to sprint down the stairs. The newly opened multiple immigration counters look impressive and more organised since my last visit. Rishab and I briefly cease our chaperoning duties and let Steve walk towards the immigration counter on his own whilst we walk to the adjacent one.

The immigration officer appears gloomy possibly unhappy to be put on night shift. He rudely snatches our passports with neatly inserted disembarkation slips even before I can place them on the counter. I get the feeling he holds us accountable for his rota.

'*Where* are you here?'' the officer demands angrily.

Rishab stops yawing fleetingly and wonders if he heard the words incorrectly.

'On visit,' I answer meekly, pleased with myself to have understood him.

He examines our passports; he pauses as he checks my photograph in the passport. He looks at me briefly and then scans the photograph once again. I try to conceal my guilt as the flattering airbrushed picture was taken nearly a decade ago. He brushes down his thick bushy moustache momentarily, shakes his head and then decides to feel charitable looking at Rishab, who has resumed his yawning and stretching exercise. I am not sure if I want our passports back after they have been handled by hands that have stroked furry germy facial hair. The officer stamps our passports with enormous power to relieve his depression. He hands us our passports with a portion of the disembarkation slips before waving us away like cattle. I am unhappy with his customer service and English speaking skills and strongly feel the need to bring it to his attention but fearing deportation and another sleepless night possibly in a prison cell, I let it pass.

We meet Steve at the baggage claim area. He is surrounded by four underpaid baggage handlers. The baggage handlers insist on taking Steve's luggage trolley in four different directions to help him claim his bag in exchange for a few American dollars. Steve has not grasped the situation and is unable to understand why his trolley is so popular. I rescue Steve and enlarge my bloodshot eyes and dismiss the harassing staff away by threatening to report them to their managers. They scamper like they have seen an evil spirit and then quickly recover to pick on another gullible foreign victim.

'Have I told you lately that you are a real treasure?' Steve says as he gives me a gentle squeeze, thankful for my timely intervention.

'Only every time we are together (!)' I joke as I try to conceal my school girl bashfulness but fail as I have lost control on most of my features. I give a 'no worries' rub on his broad shoulders and wonder if the physical contact was necessary.

We claim our bags and walk towards the exit where we are directed to put our bags through an X-ray machine by beer bellied custom officers. Steve looks completely disorientated and wonders if we have come the wrong way. He itches his prickly stubble and looks around for exit signs. Tiny beads of sweat have now formed an interesting pattern on his forehead. He stops itching and swats a huge mosquito that has settled on his neck and misses it. I sigh and speculate whether I have got more than I bargained for. Looking after a vulnerable Steve was not going to be an easy ride.

We wheel ourselves out after having our bags scanned and meet a police constable who gestures to hand him our stamped disembarkation slips. Steve has now surrendered completely to the series of peculiar encounters and appears to be in a trance.

As we make our way out of the airport, we hear sales pitches for currency exchange, taxi services and hotel bookings made by smiling and hopeful staff, caged in their individual crammed cubicles. They call Steve '*Mishterrr* James *Bhannd*'. Steve strangely understands their accent and snaps out of his trance and humbly waves at his adoring fans, thankful for his new found stardom. I am moved by their plight. I consider myself fortunate when I compare myself to these hard-working individuals who work odd hours in these dreadful conditions to sustain their families. I smile apologetically as I pass them by. They don't appear disheartened and turn their attention on another couple walking behind us. I can't help smiling at our true Indian spirit. I am happy to be back home again.

Chapter Twelve

'Natasha,' I hear a familiar voice amidst the thronging crowd of expectant relatives and friends of the arriving passengers. Some break their boredom by analysing every dead beat life form trailing out through the exit glass door. A few hold misspelt passenger names on floppy cardboard banners. A curly haired young man dressed in a grey shirt and black baggy trousers, possibly employed by a five star hotel as he bears their logo on his black tie, holds a white sheet of paper that reads Franz Schmitt. As he sees me emerge through the exit door he straightens his droopy shoulders, holds the banner above his mop of curls and smiles and looks at me with renewed vigour and optimism. I doubt if he has been briefed appropriately on nationality and gender of his new client.

As I seek the face of the familiar voice I catch sight of two wrinkly clones of Maya giving us condemnatory evils possibly mistaking Steve and me to be a couple. They exchange their thoughts as they hold their multiple sagging chins, tut and shake their heads and gawp sympathetically at Rishab.

The exit area is dimly lit by yellow neon street lights. There are numerous cars parked in the parking area across the road. But there are even more parked unlawfully in the 'no parking' zone near the exit area. A few rupees change hands for this deed. A frail police constable, an active participant in this exchange of funds, beats a wooden stick to the ground as he walks unsteadily asserting his authority in the area. He makes a loud throaty sound and projectile spits on the road. I take that as a cue to look away.

'Mum, look its Tina aunty!' Rishab says, hugely relieved that the end to his bed-less travel ordeal seems finally near.

'Is that your sister?' Steve asks, energized by the sight of an attractive woman smiling and waving her slender hands in the air at us.

'No flies on you eh Steve(!)' I say as I presume Steve could tell by the striking resemblance.

'She looks so different from you. Man, she is stunning!' Steve says, impolitely taking the shine off my only redeeming moment of this hellish journey. 'Charming(!) Don't look too surprised. What do you mean by 'different'…err…on second thoughts don't bother and put your tongue back in, will you? You'll catch mosquitoes,' I say as my heart plummets to a new low. I am annoyed with Tina for taking pride in her appearance at 3 in the morning. We watch her elegant slim figure in lime green skinny jeans teamed with a white ruffle top, walk towards us. Her thick mane of hair has been carefully coiffed to form soft curls to frame her pretty face. A hint of gloss on her full lips glistens against her flawless radiant porcelain complexion. I feel dwarfed by her frame that has been artificially elevated thanks to a pair of 'orgasmic' wedge heels. She hugs me as we air kiss. Rishab gets a kiss on his lips while Steve impatiently forms an orderly queue behind Rishab for a similar reception.

'You must be Steve. I am Tina, Natasha's sister. Welcome to Mumbai! Good to finally put a face to a name. I have heard so much about you,' Tina says as she stretches one of her French manicured hands out to Steve. Steve wets his lips and appears disproportionately disappointed. He manages a weak smile and stretches out his hand to find Tina's for a warm handshake and says, 'Pleased to meet you Tina, I have heard a lot about you too!'

'Bet you have (!)' I hear myself whisper with utter displeasure.

As Steve and Tina get acquainted, Rishab and I are left wheeling the luggage trolley on our own until Sunil, the young new recruit, immaculately uniformed family chauffer, greets me respectfully with folded hands and swiftly takes it off my hands and disappears into the parking lot. We wait for Sunil and Tina's car by a telephone booth run by two middle aged disabled men. Steve and Tina seemed to have a lot in common for people who have met just a couple of seconds ago. Rishab has discovered he can pass his time by fogging a glass window with his hot breath and scribbling his name on it. He looks pleased with this gimmick and forms more fog patches to draw caricature faces this time. I am too shattered and annoyed to stop him and look away only to end up meeting one of the disabled men's gaze. He mistakes me for a potential customer.

'Aunty, want to make a phone call you?' he asks, pointing at an unattractive grimy red phone, the size of a small refrigerator. I can hear the words tumble out of his mouth in slow motion, the word 'Aunty' in particular. I immediately look around for onlookers. It's too late. Steve, Tina and Rishab have all turned after prematurely concluding their respective activities. Uncannily, they point their right index fingers at me and repeat the word 'Aunty' in harmony, in complete sync with each other and burst into hysterics.

'Who are calling Aunty you, Granduncle?' I snap back, keeping up with the incorrect grammar, ensuring the message is well and truly received. It was strangely liberating to vent out all the grief, humiliation and frustration that I had borne during the past few hours on a complete stranger.

I turn around to face my laughing associates, 'I give you lot three seconds to compose yourselves, unless you want to become limbless and join the two men in running the booth,' I threaten as I watch Sunil park Tina's Honda Accord close to us. I storm into the back seat of the car and the three follow me like disobedient school children.

'So are you going to tell me about Priti, or is the purpose of my visit completely forgotten?' I ask Tina, still miffed with her disloyalty.

Sunil gets behind the wheels after loading our luggage. He doesn't see the need to park the trolley suitably and leaves it in the middle of the road to obstruct four vehicles behind us. Instead, he sees the need to catch up on the going-ons. He was sure he had left a merry bunch of fours and now the group seems to have split into two. He adjusts his rear view mirror to include the images of his back seat passengers. He starts the ignition, switches on the cool air-conditioner and honks for no apparent reason, in co-ordination with other passing cars. Steve who has settled in the front seat appears startled. He ducks and looks through the four windows to investigate the honking frenzy, but fails to find a conclusive motive.

'Yes, sorry. She seems to be doing well now. She is living with her parents now. Will talk later, I don't want Rishab to hear the rest,' Tina whispers into my ears.

'Of course,' I am ashamed at my outburst.

Sunil gets the car moving skilfully without checking the rear view and side mirrors. He demonstrates his driving skills further by taking his eyes off the road whilst the car is still in motion and opens a little leather flap to expose a small collection of neatly arranged CDs. Sunil appears to know what he is looking for. I get the feeling the chosen CD is for Steve's benefit. Buttons on an intense gizmo are pressed and the CD is inserted with maximum exactitude. A female Hindi playback singer sings about her lost love while a male English rap artist goes 'Oh yeaaaah'' every 10 seconds like he is on heat. Tina and I solidify unable to find a way to take charge of the situation. Rishab mercifully has no time to take in the lyrics as he has resumed tapping into his new found fog patch caricature talent, this time on the glass window. Steve in contrast is completed enthralled by the Indo-Western erotic composition. He turns behind to smile and flash his eyebrows at me. I manage a feeble smile while Tina pretends to look interested in Rishab's fine art.

We arrive at the entrance of a sprawling building. Tina and Ricky have recently moved with their sons into a four bedroom apartment just above my parents' equally large apartment. Sunil honks for an apparent reason, this time, in an attempt to wake the two sleeping security guards. They seem irritated with the unwanted interruption. But as they open the gates and recognise the car, they immediately straighten up their sluggish bodies and salute the glaring headlights unable to look past it.

Sunil whizzes the car in and screeches it to a halt just outside the lobby entrance. Pink and black polished granite flooring, gleam under numerous spotlights. A table made of the same granite material has a sleeping security guard spread all over it.

'Security is tight as ever (!),' I joke as Tina looks crossly at the lifeless being. She stomps towards sleeping beauty, picks up the visitors book placed on a swivel chair and throws it on the floor. Sleeping beauty is rudely returned to the real world from slumber land as the impact echoes through the lobby. Tina is in no mood to hear the apologies; she stomps towards the elevator and presses a huge black button.

As Sunil dutifully walks behind us with the luggage; we cram into the confined space of the elevator. The steel doors slips shut, Tina presses a button with 18 written on it. Steve looks fascinated by a little fan that has automatically switched itself on, we hear it make a loud whirring noise as it executes its task.

'Steve, I think we are best staying at Mum and Dad's as Ricky and Tina will be away most of the day, working,' I say as I sort out the accommodation arrangements.

'I am not fussed,' Steve says, looking noticeably fussed. I sense he would have rather stayed at Tina's. I observe Steve keenly gawp at Tina on the reflective steel surface of the elevator doors. Tina seems unaware of this scrutiny as she watches the little digital screen change numbers as we pass over each floor.

'Stevie, what are you thinking?' I ask as I make a sincere effort to deflect the situation.

'Hmm?' Steve looks upset with my ill-timed query as all sets of eyes in the elevator are on him.

'What's on your mind?' I rephrase my query.

Steve immediately glances at Sunil's moustache to hide his embarrassment. It's Sunil's turn to look embarrassed and he looks uneasy with the sudden attention. He smiles nervously.

'This is a bit random but why do Indian men grow moustaches? Right from all the male flight attendants, to immigration officers, to your security guards, to this gentleman here, have moustaches. Do I need to grow one as well to blend in even more?'

'*Saar*, it is sign of being a real man,' Sunil answers the question for us as he twirls his own proudly. Steve looks puzzled with the response.

'So, Stevie are you up for some luncheon at 'The Retreat' later. It's a modish hotel by the sea,' I say, baffled with myself for scheduling this arbitrary outing. Now why was I so keen to spend time with Steve alone? What was I even thinking, how could I have forgotten about Priti? I could tell the same thoughts have crossed Tina's mind as well as she raises her eyebrows at me.

'Oh yeaaah!' Steve responds, mimicking the rap artist from Bollywood remix song making Tina giggle. I glare at Steve and he looks away pleased with my reaction.

Chapter Thirteen

I am locked in a passionate embrace with a mystery man, he holds me close to his chest and I can feel his hot breath burn my skin. He strokes my hair gently and plants numerous soft kisses on them. My hair is surprisingly bouncy and glistens like women in dreamy commercials for hair shampoos and colourants. He smells fresh and strangely familiar and I like that and find it comforting. I nestle my head closer to his warm body and liquefy into his strong arms. I am enjoying the proximity too much to tear myself away to see his face. But curiosity gets the better of me and I break away unwillingly to look into his eyes. I can't seem to focus, the image is blur he shakes my weak body and opens his mouth and to my horror he speaks in Tina's voice and screeches, 'WAKE UP SLEEPYHEAD!'

I can now strangely focus my vision with amazing clarity. I am looking into Tina's pretty face. One of my limbs decides to reach for a pillow and hit her on her head with it.

'Hey, I can't believe you did that! Now look what you've done, it took me ages to get my curls sitting perfectly.' She frantically sifts through her large tan leather Prada handbag for her hairbrush. She reminds me of an over dramatic paramedic in ER who searches for the right equipment to carry out checks on a dying patient. She darts towards the wardrobe and swings open one of the doors to expose a full length mirror. She hurriedly tames her glossy tresses like they are all going to fall out any minute. She brushes the top half of her crowning glory and scrunches the soft curls at the ends with her hands. She pouts her lips and checks her hair from different angles. I begin to wonder if there is a link between pouting lips and styling hair. Maybe I should try this technique and discreetly make mental notes in my semi-conscious mind. She has worn a candy pink shift dress. I trace the outline of her trim figure through my partially opened eyes with unconditional envy and then look down at the small bulge that's hanging immodestly over the bottoms of my Minnie Mouse pyjamas. I blame Rishab for spreading himself rather too comfortable in my womb. Tina would have probably trained her unborn children to position their bodies in a way that wouldn't play havoc with her taut figure and stomach muscles.

'Go away Tina and leave me alone, I am jetlagged, tired and very cross with you for interrupting my steamy virtual romance with my aromatic mystery man. And thanks to you, I didn't get to know him or even see his face!' I go back to hugging my pillow. I try to create the same scenario and ambience with the mystery man in mind but fail as Tina starts her nagging.

'It's almost noon and your American guest who is not so virtual is in the living room waiting for his hot date. You do recall planning this luncheon with him, don't you? Care to shed some light on this little arrangement? I couldn't help noticing…the two of you seem to be very cosy. Last night you nearly bit my head off claiming I had entirely forgotten the purpose of your visit and yet you seemed to have done exactly the same thing,' Tina says as she generously gives me a throbbing headache with her whingeing. In the past few years, I have observed she has ceased flexing her facial muscles when she is in a mood with someone, fearing the appearance of unwanted premature wrinkles. It is frightening to see her angry minus the facial expressions. I reckon this approach has more impact on her victims.

'Couldn't you take him out instead? I am sure he'll be pleased with the change in plans. Now disappear and leave me alone,' I beg with sincerity as the blurry image in my mind begins to fade away quickly.

'No! And I won't until you tell me what's happening here. Your husband has let you fly with a male colleague and not just any male colleague, but one that is single and searingly good-looking as this one,' she says, pointing at the bedroom door which faces the living room, 'And why are you romancing with virtual mystery men? That is so completely immoral!' Tina says in disgust. I can sense she demands some serious answers from me. I don't understand why romancing with virtual mystery men is so upsetting and immorally wrong. Not all of us have perfect husbands like Ricky. Actually she did make a valid point. I am not sure if I am single yet, and I am already beginning to enjoy the status by fantasizing about smelling and latching on to faceless men.

'You couldn't pick another time to have this deep conversation, could you? Alright then, if you really want to know, Rakesh and I have decided to put some space between us for a bit. Please don't tell any of this to the Roys, this is not a trial separation. We just need some time to iron out a few issues. Steve is here to get away from a personal setback. And there is 'nothing' going on between Steve and me. I am not his type anyway,' I shrug, feeling pitiful after a brief reality check.

'Space? Issues? I don't understand. What are you on about? Speaking of Rakesh...the poor man has left umpteen messages. Could you at least return his calls? I've informed him that you've all arrived in one piece...though I am not so sure about you,' she says, looking at my disjointed body sprawled over two pillows. 'I am late for work, we are not done yet. I'll catch you later. And please do something with your hair!' she reprimands me as she picks a dry lock of my hair and leaves it standing with my other 'Freddies'. Freddy is a name I have lovingly christening each of my hair strands that stand on their ends and defy gravity, come whatever the weather.

I emerge from my room after a quick shower looking pretty much like I did before hitting the sack. I glance across the living room. Steve, Mr and Mrs Roy are in conversation about the American economy. Steve's pet hate subject, primarily due to lack of knowledge. I glance at the carved wooden Jaipur table. Steve has been made to consume dainty pastries, greasy Indian savouries and strong cups of Indian spiced tea, probably against his will. There is an abrupt silence as they turn around to look my way. Steve has never looked happier to see me. The Roys appear uncomfortable with my entry. I begin to wonder if it is the inappropriate interruption into the one-sided conversation or my shabby appearance to be blamed.

'Don't mind me, please continue,' I say, to gloss over the apparent awkwardness.

'Would you like to join us or do you want to have your breakfast at the table?' mother asks, dressed elegantly in a sea blue chiffon sari, concerned to get some food into me, as always.

'Nah…it's too late for breakfast. Besides, I am taking Steve out for a quick tour of the city…will grab some lunch on the way. Has Rishab woken up yet?' I ask as I look around for the round imp.

'He insisted on joining Tina when he overheard her mentioning a photo shoot with Yana Gupta,' *Pa* chuckles and looks at Steve who is unable to get the joke. 'Kids today, they start so young!'

'*Pa*! I am glad it tickles you to find that your grandson has a crush on a woman three times his age, when we weren't even allowed to bring home glossy magazines,' I jog Mr Roy's memory and take him back in time when he was an absolute tyrant, obsessive about protecting his daughters' innocence.

'But I thought you said your parents were/are liberal minded,' Steve says, starting to keep pace with the conversation. The Roys look surprised and pleased to be fashionably labelled as liberal minded by their rebellious daughter.

Before Steve can spring further surprises and divulge and discuss finer points from our private conversations, I take the Roys leave. We are given the family car and the services of Pa's chauffer for the grand city tour. We willingly take the car but decide to ditch *Pa's* trusty but an excessively depressive chauffeur. I've known him since I was about three, but I have yet to see him smile. He has had a hard life and doesn't miss an opportunity to remind us about it. It has been a long time since I have driven on the mean streets of Mumbai and for some bizarre reason, I realise I have missed the recklessness of driving dangerously.

'Are we heading towards the 'modish' hotel or are you going to surprise me by taking me somewhere else?' Steve queries as he struggles to contain his excitement. 'I can't believe you can still drive here, I am well impressed!'

I am well pleased that he is well impressed and I quickly conceal my fear of being on the other side of the road. This is not my only worry. Since the time we'd set off, I have been trying to shake off two rickshaws which seem to be practically glued on either side of our car. These little black and yellow three tyred motor scooters are fast becoming the city's preferred public transport. They have been multiplying at an alarming rate in the past few years. Judging by the driving skills, I am not sure if you need a driver's licence to operate these little devils. One of these motors is probably hired for the school run. I do a quick head count and find eight tiny bodies packed like sardines carrying their overloaded school bags and water bottles on their tiny backs. They all appear to be in intense conversations despite being in various yogic postures and constant vibratory motion.

The other rickshaw has a young couple making out at the back, much to the amusement of its driver. The driver looks through his strategically placed numerous rear view mirrors and has a Big Brother reality show of his own in motion. Engrossed with the steamy back seat action, he loses focus and takes a detour knocking off one of our side mirrors in the process.

'Oooiii!' I scream and honk simultaneously. The rickshaw driver brakes and parks his rusty heap next to our car. I wind down the glass window using the power button. The heat and stench of cheap booze hits my face. I quickly begin to mentally rehearse my sentences with sprinkling of just the right amount of abuses in Hindi. The driver looks uglier and bigger up close. Road accidents in India are dealt differently. The concerned parties threaten dire consequence and if need be carry out the threats and then each go their separate ways. I threaten to have him beaten up by my foreign bodyguard. He lowers his ugly mug to look at Steve. He starts laughing like a sinister villain in a Z-grade film. I can't help noticing the young couple haven't ceased showing their affections to each other.

I turn around hoping to catch Steve flexing his strong muscles, instead I find him looking terrified unable to come to terms with his recent experience. However, he has managed to find a piece of paper and pen to scribble the registration number. The driver hasn't stopped laughing and I am now beginning to feel equally terrified. I don't like the thought of feeling defeated. I look around the car, rev up the engine and reach for the florescent yellow car duster over the glove compartment. I swing it wildly hitting the laughing brute and step on the accelerator.

Chapter Fourteen

I drive towards the entrance of 'The Retreat' when a Sikh valet lunges in front of the car in an eager pursuit to open my car door. I break prematurely and stop 100 yards away from the main entrance. The valet greets me with a frightening smile revealing a set of teeth which are in different stages of decaying process. I begin to worry if this image is going to stay with me whilst I lunch.

'Good day Madam,' he says as he holds the door open for her majesty to alight and hand over the car keys. I quickly forgive the valet for giving me brief nauseating thoughts and begin to enjoy the royal treatment and graciously surrender the keys. As Steve and I walk towards the lobby we hear the car screech angrily as it is being recklessly driven away by the seemingly mild natured valet.

'This is nice,' Steve says as he generously seals his stamp of approval sounding almost surprised that the place has lived up to the hype. He greedily surveys the reception area where a group of young girls in skimpy tops and minute skirts have crowded together to check-in. I conclude there is a pattern, a cult of some sort within this coterie. They look like clones of each other. I suspect Steve doesn't see them that way. He takes his time to trail his eyes on each of the stick insects, with his tongue hanging loose over his lower lip.

Hair, cut to similar length, straightened with styling irons and set with industrial strength serums and hairsprays, the groupies bounce with enormous energy. I begin to almost doubt if they have coiled metal springs attached under the soles of their footwear. They squeak with replicated shrill voices declaring and celebrating their escapism from traditional and objecting families. Maniacal text messages are fired off to imaginary parties from their tiny mobile phones whist still in mid air. One of the numpties slows down her bounce as she glances at Steve. She whispers to her clan and they turn around and burst into flirtatious giggles. They flick their straightened rigid hair in hope of some foreign excitement. What disturbs me is that that they don't look at me as competition. In fact I get the feeling I am invisible to the genetically identical life forms. I yank the salivating Steve's sleeve and drag his protesting body towards the restaurant.

As we enter the restaurant, I catch sight of a small gang of waiters huddled in a corner. They exchange opinions on first impressions of their potential clienteles as I am still clutching one of Steve's sleeves. My reflex releases the sleeve from my grasp. The verdict doesn't seem favourable. They snigger overtly.

'We hate to break the party...table for two, in your own time (!), please.' I say as I target my eyes at the ring master.

'Sure sure, Madam, come this way,' the ring master unsuccessfully rearranges his face to appear more hospitable. He would be in his early thirties and has an unusually large belly for a thin frame. I presume like me 'exercising' isn't his thing. Like his little syndicate he has worn a white shirt, a black bow tie and a red vest on a pair of black trousers.

We are given a table with two chairs facing each other, overlooking the hotel pool and a large lawn. Steve now looks officially impressed.

The ring master hands me a menu card even before our tired bottoms make contact with the dark wooden seats. We leave him holding out the card until we comfortably settle ourselves in. I reach for the card and scan the extensive menu with one very brief glance whilst Steve wonders why he isn't given a menu to do the same.

'Shall we have a drink before we order lunch?' I suggest to Steve who has now diverted his attention to a very wet and a very voluptuous young woman in an animal print bikini, emerging from the pool. Steve gazes at her as she dabs her curves with a soft white towel. I am surprised to find my fingernails digging into my chair. Could this be a sign of jealously or annoyance? But why would I be envious of anyone getting Steve's attention. I put my money on annoyance.

'Grrrrr Tiger,' Steve roars in whispers as he is floating away in a dreamy bubble that takes him through the glass pane into the arms of the Indian mermaid. I find the hotel waiter has joined him in this virtual air borne flight.

'Ahem...' I pretend to clear my throat in an attempt to bring Steve and the waiter back to the real world. I fail. I could try shouting but that would disturb the diners.

'AAAAAtttchhhhoooo,' a pretend sneeze works every time. Steve and the waiter look at me annoyed and disgusted as they lose sight of their muse who has now melted away into the changing room.

'Oops sorry...bless me...shall we have a drink before we order lunch?' I repeat the question nonchalantly quite pleased with my clever approach.

'Go on then, I could murder a bottle of chilled beer...what's the name of the Indian beer that's named after a bird?' Steve asks the waiter who doesn't respond. He holds on to a small notepad and pen motionlessly. I am not quite sure if the word 'murder' is responsible for his current state.

'Kingfisher!' I say, breaking the spell.

It works. 'Yes, yes sir. We have 'very good' chilled Kingfisher beer,' the waiter says, fancying a quick gulp of it himself. He scribbles on his notepad and then turns to me.

'And Madam?'

'Orange Juice for me for now, and we'll place the order for the meal a bit later. Thank you,' I say, in an attempt to close the order. The waiter doesn't scribble my order into his notepad. Instead he looks at me hopefully to elaborate on my order. Steve raises his eyebrows high enough to meet his hairline and joins the waiter for further definition.

'Madam small, medium or large?' The waiter asks as he holds out his notepad in anticipation.

'Large please.'

'With or without ice Madam?'

'With ice, please.'

'Smooth or with juicy bits Madam?'

'Smooth please,' I say as I bite my lower lip, I am not sure if I can endure this grilling interrogation any longer.

'Madam, we have the Indian brand and the American Tropicana, which one would you prefer?'

'I would prefer you to get me one glass of orange juice. Is that too much to ask?' I shriek, dehydrated with the pressured cross examination. Steve looks embarrassed to be sat at the same table as me as he watches the other diners who have their jaws dropped to the ground to reveal semi masticated food in their mouths, blatantly interested in the drama.

'No, absolutely not, Madam. Please accept my apologies, one chilled bottle of Kingfisher for Sir and one orange juice with ice for you Madam.' The gruelling interrogator quickly scribbles the order into his notepad and quickly disappears.

Steve throws his head back and then immediately brings it forward to rest it between his hands on the table. He looks fed up and worn out like the Basset hound dog of Hush Puppies after numerous photo shoots. Like the worrisome canine, Steve wonders if things can get any worse, 'Good grief! Is there no stopping you? How does the poor doctor put up with you? You have got to credit the man for his endurance. You are luckier than you think woman!'

'Yeah, I keep reminding myself every time I pick his underpants from the floor (!)' I say, miffed with men and the unwavering solidarity they show to their own kind.

The mobile phone that Tina kindly gifted exclusively for my stay begins to ring almost as a sign of agreement to my thoughts. I pick it up to answer it only I don't know how. But what I do know is that I don't recognise the number. I rapidly begin to show signs of embarrassment and panic when Steve seizes it from my hand and effortlessly presses a button and hands it back to me but not before shaking his head with sheer disbelief.

'Hello?' I ask hesitatingly.

'Nuts?' answers a male voice. Did I hear the word right; I question myself repeatedly for four seconds.

'Nuts? Hello Nuts, is that you?' asks the defiant voice.

Yes there was no mistaking, I did hear it right.

'I am afraid you have got the wrong number unless it's your idea of some kind of a sick joke, Mister!'

'It's Veer Shroff you idiot!!'

Chapter Fifteen

'OH-MY-GOD!!!! I screech, with a laboured nasal American accent, sounding frighteningly parallel to Janice from 'Friends' coupled with her irritating laughter. I can barely contain my excitement like a frenzied fan who has spotted her favourite Bollywood star and prefer to exhibit this emotion by bouncing up and down like the girls in the reception area. I go a step further and add a different dimension to the bounce by performing this feat on the wooden chair. I run my fingers through my hair and tease it unconsciously as I wet my lips. I am not certain why I have lost control over my senses. I should know better that Veer could only hear my voice.

'I'll be damned....Veeeeeer Shroooofffffff! How are you? Where have you been? How did you get my number?' I ask hysterical with this bizarre unexpected call.

There were so many questions swimming in my head, I catch my breath to sort them in the order of importance. I notice that I have attracted the attention from other diners once again for all the wrong reasons. A bit like the young father behind Steve's handsome head. The father with two overloaded baby bags strapped across his chest, possibly carrying a kitchen sink in one of them, struggles to unleash his toddler from the restaurant's crudely made high chair. The struggle intensifies as the toddler's nappy has grown in size as a result of an unwise liquid diet. A lolly is thrust into the child's mouth as a precautionary measure for any foreseeable wails. The unscrupulous grinning waiter-syndicate organise a 'spur-of-the-moment' sweepstake on timescales on the father's misfortune.

The mother appears lethargic and in no mood to lend a helping hand after a good meal. Young urban city mothers in India are a far cry from those a few decades ago. Elaborate saris or *salwar kameez* and even more elaborate dotted foreheads are replaced with tight jeans and tighter T-shirts. Saris are now worn by city dwelling nouveau westernised women on traditional occasions and a preferred safe attire whilst visiting conservative in-laws. Like her generation today, this young mother is no different. Although this one appears to have worn her toddler's T-shirt. Her breasts seemed to have lost their shape after being cruelly squeezed into the tiny top. As she swings her gold handbag to sling it on her shoulder she reveals a network of postnatal stretch marks on her soft brown belly. I gasp and shut my eyes and temporarily forget the sequence my questions I aimed to fire at Veer as she turns around audaciously to reveal her butt crack. What is it about today's women and low jeans? A sight that would have brought 'shame' and 'dishonour' to the young woman's family and her dead ancestors a few years ago, but today people prefer to notice my bounce and not her butt crack that's in full view.

The 'cheeky' woman displays her skills in excavating remnants of her meal stuck between her teeth with her long fingernails. She decides she can multitask and hovers around our table to piece together bits of my tele-talk. Staring and listening into private conversations are hot leisure pursuits in India. The USP being it's free, entertaining and comforting to watch someone else having a worse day than you. The tooth excavation expert swans off as her heaving husband and I fall short of keeping her engaged in our individual performances.

Our absconding waiter brings in the drinks, mine in a glass that matches my height with a pink cocktail paper umbrella floating proudly on the juice. The waiter shifts the condiments and a vase containing two flowers on its last legs, to the far edge of the table. He places two similar wooden coasters on our table. Quite content with this new arrangement, he places my drink on one of the coasters. He places an empty beer glass on the other coaster that's close to Steve. He then holds an unopened beer bottle by its neck and tucks away the empty tray under his armpit.

He displays the beer label by titling the bottle at Steve. Steve at this point is not sure if has ordered a precious bottle of vintage Indian wine. He leans forward and reads the label and is quickly reassured. The waiter breaks into a broad smile on receiving a positive indication from Steve and wastes no time to whip out a gleaming silver bottle opener from a cleverly hidden pocket on his vest. The metal cap is released skilfully demonstrating high proficiency in beer bottle opening. Steve appears stupefied until the waiter pours 10 ml of the golden frothy liquid into the empty beer glass. The waiter steps aside holding the bottle close to his chest for further affirmations. Steve eventually receives the message and obediently drinks the frugally poured drink. He nods appreciatively fearing disappearance of the bottle. The positive gesture initiates the waiter to fill Steve's glass until the white froth touches the rim of the glass. Steve gulps air as he can sense he is moments away from attaining nirvana, I should have known Steve's idea of spiritual journey was different from mine. The waiter leaves us alone after placing the menu card underneath the condiments and vase.

A grandfather dining at a 'table for six' with his grandson has a banquet spread in front of him, yet he eyes our drinks curiously. I have often wondered why diners seem more interested in food and drinks on other tables rather than their own.

'Easy, easy, easy…one question at a time. I am good. Studied photography in the US…went back packing….which took me to Australia…and eventually back to my roots. I have been here for four years and now into Fashion photography….a legend in the business as it happens!' he says.

'Of course (!) I couldn't possibly expect any less from you (!)' I add.

'I met Tina through work just a couple of months ago,' He continues 'I am surprised she hasn't spoken about me, because we did speak about you. It wasn't hard to recognise Tina after all this time….Foxy Lady!!!!' he says, sounding inappropriately lusty.

'Careful, that's my sister you are referring to, in case you need reminding.' I say, upset with Veer's choice of words.

'Chill...only winding you up, you idiot! Believe me I did want to get in touch....anyway we'll talk when we meet. Priti's mum called a couple of days ago....you do know about Priti, don't you?'

'Yes...yes.' I confirm and bounce solemnly.

'And I just thought of you...remembering how close the two of you were. I got in touch with Tina just moments ago and hey Presto! It's good to hear your voice again....no evolution there... you sound daffffttttt as ever! Bet you have loads of wrinkles and grey hair though!' Veer chuckles. Veer has always laughed the loudest at his own jokes, a perfected defence mechanism lest they failed to generate a desired response. My bounce abruptly terminates on hearing Veer's last few words.

'Speak for yourself, you moron!' I say, putting on a phoney American accent again, Steve looks amused. He hasn't stopped smiling since my 'Janice' impersonation.

'Relax....was only joking. Uptight as ever! Listen...I was thinking... I feel a bit awkward visiting Priti on my own after all these years...I haven't seen her since the time she got married... and with the present circumstances...do you want to come with me, maybe we could hook up before that? You could join me for a drink this evening?' he suggests.

'I haven't seen her either since she got married...today is a bit short notice. Can I take a rain check on that? Or...hang on a minute...how about tomorrow evening?' I make an executive decision as I don't want this chance meeting with Veer to slip away. Shouldn't I be more concerned about meeting Priti?

'Fab...suits me. How about sevenish at Lou's Blues?'

'Lou's Blues? What is that? Where 'louussers' like you hangout?' I burst into flirtatious giggles like the reception numpties.

'Idiot! It's a pub! Tina tells me you are in Retreat...that's where the pensioners hangout!' Veer retaliates with another well timed fictitious chuckle.

'You know I am not too keen on being called an 'Idiot' every two seconds unless you want to visit Priti on your own!' We have been barely on the phone for five minutes after a gap of nearly twenty years and we have picked off from where it had all ended, engaging in pointless banter.

I compose myself and stop entwining clumps of hair around my index finger when I see Steve raise his left eyebrow suspiciously. I feel guilty and responsible for neglecting his presence. He hasn't touched his drink since the waiter filled his glass as I haven't touched mine. I mouth an apology without saying it aloud. But he is having none of it. The eyebrow remains static.

'Okay, okay, okay…Veer I have got to go now. I am in the midst of having lunch with a friend…just text me the address and I'll be there at 'sevenish'. See you tomorrow. Byeeee!' I wave my hand in the air living up to the title of an 'Idiot'. To cement this further I hand the phone across to Steve to help me press the right button.

'If the caller has hung up, you needn't bother ending the call.' Steve says wearily.

I check the tiny screen and am relieve to see the name of the service provider.

'I am so so sorry….you could have made a start with your drink…awww were you waiting for me to end the call? That is so sweet!' I raise my glass. 'Cheers…to Steve…my special friend,' I say, bringing the glass to my mouth forgetting the presence of the floating pink umbrella until it touches my nose and on impact folds itself up and propels into my right nostril.

'Cheers!…Hormonal patches wearing off!…eh Tash?' Steve says as he gulps down his flat drink.

'What do you mean?' I ask as I craftily extricate the umbrella like it is an everyday occurrence.

'Who is Veeeeeer Shrawoooofffffff? 'A Blast from the Past'? How come you have never spoken about this person…I am presuming he is a 'special' 'male' friend…since I have never seen you like this before,' Steve says, looking slightly upstaged.

'Phhhffff…nonsense…'A Blast from the Past' indeed. What

a vivid imagination! And it's 'Veer Shroff'....I've mentioned this before, sadly there has only ever been Rakesh for me. Veer said he got my number from Tina. And Tina knows we were good friends and yet she chose not to update me on her various encounters with him. Apparently they have worked together on a few assignments. It doesn't make sense. She has got a lot of explaining to do. Aaarrrghhh ...honestly sometimes she can be so wrapped up in her candy floss world.' I growl as I show my frustration by clenching my fists. Steve looks worried.

'Calm down Tash...here have my fizzless beer if it helps,' Steve jokes as he pushes his glass towards me.

'No thanks...I am alright...besides I am driving, remember?' I politely decline the offer and push the glass back to Steve. It wasn't the driving, it was the glass that Steve had already drunk from. How could I drink someone else's bacteria and go through life.

'Veer was a special friend...yes....but we grew apart and he preferred to disappear to pursue photography and have never heard from him since...it's been nearly twenty years now. Gosh! I feel like a fossil. It's been so long. Hey...we are meeting up tomorrow...why don't you come with me and find out for yourself what you think of him?' I say as I press Steve's hand.

'Nawwh...I don't know. You guys obviously seem close and are meeting up after years ...I don't want to play gooseberry!' Steve pulls his hand away slowly in a way not to offend me.

'It's not a 'romantic' meeting for you to play gooseberry. I really would want you to meet him....besides it's a choice between a night out with us or a night in with Mr & Mrs Roy discussing global credit crunch and recession.'

'Well if you put it like that...a night 'in' it is then...no, only kidding...go on, since you've twisted my arm and I am strangely intrigued by this mysterious 'special' friend.' I suspect a hint of sarcasm attached to the word 'special'.

'Can I ask you something?' he asks.

'Sounds ominous (!)...Fire away!' I say.

'How would you define 'special' because there seems to figure a fair lot of individuals in this exclusive category,' Steve asks looking straight at me. In other situations I would have found the faint white froth settled on his upper lip distracting, but at this moment his liquid azure eyes have my undivided attention. It is strange how I have never noticed the colour of his eyes before.

'Just a couple...why?' I mouth unable to bear the tension. It is always good practice to keep a calm exterior and to end the sentence with an open ended question in similar situations. I score 15-Love.

'No reason...except...never mind. I am starving and I fear this drink is going to make me say things I am going to live to regret, so are you going to help me order a greasy curry or what?' he asks, making less eye contact as he gingerly tries to slide away the menu underneath the vase and condiments.

Just as we are faced with a challenging dilemma of selecting dishes from a palatable menu, we hear grandpa next door let out a reverberating burp. He lovingly strokes his belly and soothes it from an imminent indigestion. His little grandson seems equally appreciative of the four course meal they have just demolished between themselves and declares, 'I need a poo now!'

Chapter Sixteen

Steve and I crawl back home beaten, battling peak time
thronging Mumbai traffic and torrential downpour. I escort
and abandon Steve in Tina's apartment and deposit him in
the capable hands of Tina's sons. I ring my parents' apartment
door bell and I am greeted by an unfamiliar face. Mother does
the honours and introduces me to her beautician, Sonia. Tina,
having had an oxygen deprived nightmare starring her sister in
a solo performance looking her scruffiest best, has conjured up
this living being to work her miracle on me. Grooming to me has
been a waste of time. However, at the giddy prospect of meeting
Veer, I find myself succumbing into the opulent pleasures of
self indulgence like most Indian women. Hiring the services
of enterprising mobile beauticians and personal trainers has
become a growing weekly obsession in India.

Sonia and I get off on the wrong foot. Wheeling her portable
kit in a large trolley bag, she frogmarches me to my room, and
locks me in with her. She impolitely unplugs the table lamp and
plugs in an electrical aluminium hair removal wax melter. She
folds up her long sleeves and multiple clicks her fingers in quick
succession instructing me to strip off all my clothes. I fleetingly
look at the wax simmer sitting angrily on the bedside table.
Detecting a commanding personality, with a strong possibility
of subjecting dire consequences, I do as I am told.

'Could I at least leave my undergarments on?' I plead behind
the opened wardrobe door. She rolls her eyes and shakes her
head. I take that as a no. She walks across the room, drags me
out of my hideout and examines my skin texture by pinching
my cheek. I am too terrified to yelp.

'You don't bleach?' she inquires as she lifts my chin and holds my face up against artificial light. I am unsure whether this is an oral observation or a query.

'Err...no,' I say, which generates a series of tuts at different decibel levels. I resist the temptation to voice my opinion and say unlike her, I don't fancy blonde facial hair on olive skin.

Fair skin fixation is probably one of many aftermaths of European colonization. Fair skinned women in India are considered beautiful albeit their features do not support the definition. Fairness creams and facial bleaches have a huge niche market here; commercials for these products are aired featuring leading Bollywood movie stars depicting boyfriends dumping dusky girlfriends for fairer models. The spurned girls reach for the revolutionary fairness creams which inevitably help them conquer their men.

Matrimonial columns boast advertisements placed by mystery grooms 'seeking' young, *fair*, tall, slim, good looking and 'homely' (by which they mean unpaid slaves) girls.

'Madam, you have mature skin. When was the last time you've had a facial?' she probes further. She demands to know the truth as she prepares a mental case history on her new client.

I want to honour her professional questioning and answer truthfully and say, 'Never!' but lie and say, 'Six months ago,' as I fear another pinch and possibly a stinging slap on the other cheek.

She drops herself on the bed, stunned with the unashamed response. I lean my exposed body over the frozen figure. I wonder if I'll waste time wearing my clothes before resuscitation. Thankfully she moves slowly and reaches for her mobile phone. She cancels her other appointments for the evening as her services are required for an 'emergency' situation.

Tina pays us a nocturnal visit the same evening to check on her latest project. I am in too much pain to move from my bed. The ruthless beautician had mercilessly gone over each pore of my aching body to pull out every resisting hair. She blasted steam on my face with hose pipes used by fire fighters, she scrubbed my sore skin with green grunge that on close inspection looked and smelt like damp moss and then covered my entire body with tar which she insisted was organic seaweed. I passed out when she focused her attention on my crowning glory.

'Look at you...haven't you scrubbed up well?' Tina says as she inspects Sonia's efforts after switching on all the lights in the room. I cover my eyes with four pillows.

'You know you could at least warn me before turning on the lights in a dark room!' I begin to uncover my blinded eyes, chucking one pillow at a time in different directions in hope that one of them would hit Tina.

'Hey, that's not how I would have liked to be thanked!' Tina giggles as she picks the pillows and aims them straight at my hairless body.

'Veer had rung me today. Why didn't you tell me that you've been in touch with him?' I ask as I quickly get accustomed to the glaring lights to read Tina's face. She stops smiling and shooting pillows at me unceremoniously.

'What's wrong? Did you break a nail?' I ask, with insincere compassion, secretly hoping she did.

'I don't want you mixing with the likes of him,' she commands, ticking me off instantly.

'I'll be the judge of that. Why? What's he done? You hung out with us in the past and as I vividly recall you were very fond of him.'

Tina hesitates to explain the reason behind her brutal character assassination and abruptly leaves the room. She ensures Rishab is quickly despatched off for a sleepover with his cousins. A few minutes later she glides back into the room after growing something underneath her T-shirt. She seems to have one of her hands around this new growth. She shuts the door gently and locks it with the free hand. It's twice today I've been locked in the room by women. Tina gradually reveals a bottle of sparkling white wine and two flute glasses all hidden under one snug T-shirt and holds them up in the air like a naughty school girl.

Mr and Mrs Roy disapprove of us drinking even in our middle

age. I am curious to find out how she plans to get rid of the empty bottle and glasses. But even more curious to find out what Veer has been up to. She pours the wine in equal proportions into the crystal flutes. She hands me my drink and sips hers stylishly. I attempt to hold the flute stem in similar fashion and spill half my drink on my face. Tina rolls her eyes and shakes her head like Sonia. I wipe off the excess spillage with the sleeve of my pyjama top. Tina sits with a propped pillow behind her, legs elegantly folded to one side, her back straight as a ramrod. I prefer to sit hunched and cross legged.

'Don't get me wrong, I was fond of the guy. But he isn't the same person we once knew. Apparently the industry buzz is that he struggled to find work in the US and later in Australia. He found his way back to India a few years ago and through friends set foot into the fashion industry. Since then, he has scaled great heights. I am the first to admit, the man's got talent and is not afraid to experiment, which is refreshing,' *I sense a 'but' at this point.* 'I am not being a prude,' she continues 'but...' *there you go (!)* 'he's a womaniser and an alcoholic!' Tina proclaims as she takes a large sip of wine from her flute glass 'In fact his wife walked out on him when she found him in their bedroom, spread over a nineteen year old! And I have seen and heard him speak about other women. He is vile! I have even caught him looking sideways at my tuch! How disgusting!' Tina says, looking every inch a prude.

'Tina! Everyone looks at your tuch.' I say as I am guilty of it too.

Tina looks at me with genuine horror and pours herself some more wine. I continue 'I think you are being unfair and over-judgemental here. You know how the industry works. I mean, you of all people should know better. Veer was ambitious and egotistical, his self confidence must have taken a bashing after struggling hard to get a break for years and even harder to fit in after having to lick his wounds and come back to India as a failure.'

'Helllooo...so you are telling me he lacks confidence which gives him the right to disrespect women? You are making no sense for a wife of a psychologist,' Tina dismisses my theory with a wave of her hand.

'No! I am just saying, perhaps having women swoon over him is one way of making him feel adequate,' Tina doesn't look convinced as she begins to shake her head vigorously and I begin to dread it might detach itself from her body any second. 'So who was he married to?' I quickly change gear.

'Tanya, exquisitely beautiful and four inches taller than Veer, heard from the grapevine that she was his assistant and they had been living together for a while,' Tina's scandalised eyes widen.

Even though this is a progressive concept for Indian couples to discover the degree of their compatibility and experiment with fun and adventure before they settle down to a more domesticated arrangement, I am not quite sure if India is ready for it yet. Or is it just me? Having lived away from home for so long, for me India is what it was twelve years ago. Has time stood still for me? This one is a shocker but I conceal my old-fashioned views with a monosyllabic 'Oh (!)' as I swirl my drink and smell it like an Oenophile. Television channel surfing does have its uses.

'They married three years ago but their marriage lasted just six months. They were even gifted a comfortable three-bedroom apartment in a trendy upmarket suburb by his father. After their divorce, Tanya got the apartment and Veer got the boot. His mother stood by Tanya and disowned him completely. Presently he lives in a rented flat not far from Tanya. He's now focused and tuned into his career and women, maintaining a 'healthy' balance of business and pleasure,' Tanya says.

'I vaguely recall Veer telling me that his parents had separated after his father's infidelity. Veer's antics would have opened up his mother's old wounds, it's no wonder she wants nothing to do with him. Stupid, stupid boy. I'll speak some sense into him. I am meeting him tomorrow...'

'You most certainly are NOT!' she says as if she means business. Her eyeballs have travelled to the inner corners of her eyes. Cross-eyed, she quickly mellows and talks to my pillow, inebriated with four sips of white wine. 'And if you do, please don't let him know what I've just shared with you.'

'It's all your fault, why did you give him my number if you didn't want him anywhere near me?' *I had a point.*

'I don't know, yeah it was stupid of me to have done that. He just caught me at a wrong time,' she giggles.

'I am curious alright. You don't know him like I do. Let's just drop it. I'll meet him and if you think I need protecting, I am taking Steve with me,' I close the subject.

'It's your decision. I can't stop you,' Tina looks into her glass intently. She enjoys the little bubbles rise up to the surface and burst in her pretty drunken face.

'What are your thoughts on Steve?' I reckon this is a good time to get Tina unravel her 'inner thoughts'.

'Gorgeous, hunky, chunky, brawny, sexy…' she says, dreamily smiling at the bubbles.

'Really? Sexier than Ricky?' I am relishing this. I stop drinking; I want to remain sober to soak up the revelations.

'Way sexier! I have caught him looking at my tuch and quite enjoyed the attention!' She drinks the bubbles she was smiling at earlier.

'How disgusting!' I mouth her exact words. I decide I am not interested in her inner thoughts on Steve or Steve's inner thoughts on her. 'Okay, now tell me about Priti,' I change track skilfully.

'Priti! To be honest her mother sounded really upset and I didn't want to upset her further by probing for more explicit information. From what I gather Priti wants to end her marriage,' Tina lets out a loud unsuppressed burp. She doesn't excuse herself and appears strangely liberated with her new etiquette-less attitude. She smiles at the pillow which seems to have taken my place.

'By ending her life? I am so going to finish the job for her when I see her! Did she even stop to think about the implications this would have on her daughter or her ageing parents? I can't imagine life being that unbearable with Deepak. Deepak and

Priti looked so right for each other...' I stop my ramblings when I hear a muffled thud. Tina, still holding her empty flute glass fashionably by its stem with her thumb, index and middle fingers, has her face buried on the pillow she was talking to seconds ago.

Chapter Seventeen

Winds lash at 200 mph, the view outside my bedroom window is straight out of Steven Spielberg's 'Twister' film only it's far worse as the heavy rains come crashing down crippling and paralysing the buzzing vibrant city. Television and radio presenters beseech city folks to stay indoors. It's all doom and gloom for me as my heart takes a nose dive at the same speed as the gusty winds.

Never before had I made an earnest effort to spruce up myself. I'd rummaged through piles of designer-wear cast offs from Tina's photo shoots worn by models for 1/10th of a second and eventually settled for a sleeveless Parisian retro chic midnight blue number. I'd curled my hair with styling tongs, burning my ears, hair and scalp in the process.

'Scooooby Dooooo he he heee,' I hear Scooby's infamous laughter as a message gets transmitted into my mobile phone inbox. I foresee the dreaded text message from Veer cancelling the much awaited rendezvous. It reads '*Shal v D5 F8? I wan2 mET if u r stil up for it. SYS!*' It takes me ten minutes to decipher the cryptic text abbreviations.

I waste no time replying Veer with '*I'm on my way. SYS!*' Pleased to have trendily used a text abbreviation, I intercom Steve to meet me downstairs in a few minutes. I show my gratitude to Tina and mother for looking after Rishab two nights in a row, by sticking my head into the kitchen and blowing brief kisses in their direction. Mother doesn't reciprocate and looks at me like one would at a 'wayward' child. Tina shows her condemnation by sticking her head into the refrigerator.

Steve has settled himself in the back seat of Mr Roy's car and is in the midst of an intense sign language conversation with the chauffeur, whose English vocabulary constitutes of - thank you, yes-yes, no-no. Steve is energetically pointing towards the sky and executing swaying motions with his long arms simultaneously, the chauffeur looks up for clues to help him interpret and decode the gestures.

'Tash! You've got legs!' Steve says, appearing visibly startled and abruptly brings both his arms to his sides. I join him in the car showing off my polished pair of waxed hairless legs, deliberately exposing them in my knee length dress. 'I thought this wasn't a 'romantic' meeting,' he says, looking seriously suspicious.

'It isn't!' I say, putting Steve's worst fears to rest unsuccessfully.

'Kohl smouldering eyes and sexy legs, a fatal combination for any weak-hearted man,' Steve says, rubbing his neck and whispering into my ears. It is characteristic of Steve to rub his neck when he anticipates excitement.

'Would the word 'married' help dilute the scenario for feeble men?' I say, oscillating my left hand that wears my solitaire diamond wedding ring at Steve, pretending to tease him as I battle with my emotions. I am unsure if I am being swept away by the unidirectional undercurrents within the confines of the car or by the multidirectional squall winds outside.

I can't help feeling keyed up like a glamorised storm-catching Indian Helen Hunt with Steve besides me. Only Steve doesn't appear to be as brave and defiant as Bill Paxton. Steve's visual assessment is rudely interrupted by a gust of wind which rocks our sturdy 1.8 litre car. Our bodies collide and Steve disappears from sight. My well engineered curls adhere themselves to the gloss on my lips. Steve's mangled body lies beneath my legs. I free my curls by which time Steve re-emerges, appearing rattled like he has seen memorable moments of thirty odd years of his life flash in front of him in ten seconds.

'We must be mad…no, wait let me rephrase that, you are mad to drag me out in this weather. It's like a ghost town here. Look there's not a single car in sight!!' Steve says, furiously first repeatedly hitting his head and then pointing at a flooded deserted street ahead of us. He is breathing faster and gulping air more than usual. The view ahead bears more resemblance to 'Waterworld' than 'Twister'.

'Relax Steve, I have grown up in this city. We'll be fine, trust me,' I say, sounding incredibly unconvincing.

Merry street children exploit high walls to dive into the water logged streets, some buoyant bodies splash about wildly unable to control their pleasures. In complete contrast, a defeated couple wade through neck deep water grudgingly, holding their windswept feather light umbrella over their heads.

The chauffer floats the car which chokes and spits putrid drainage water as it sputters unwillingly to our destination. Steve and I descend from the car as the chauffeur holds his tent-sized black umbrella over us. Steve decides he doesn't require shielding from the rains. His bigger worries are the numerous puddles that have formed within the crevices of the cobbled pub entrance. He jumps to avoid falling into a pool of water but ends up leaping into a bigger and deeper one.

With no doorman in sight we find ourselves pushing a heavy resistant wooden door and tumble into the pub. I take a few steps with caution and then reach out to hold Steve's hand as the room is so dimly lit that I am unable to see further than my own nose. Steve is surprised with the sudden familiarity and grips my hand firmly to pull me closer next to him. As we encroach further we attract attention from vacant faces, who stare at us warily.

We spot two men perched on bar stools. One of them jumps off from the stool to approach us. He stops two feet away and smiles. He has a receding hairline but a flourishing pair of eyebrows and day old stubble.

'Natasha! Glad you could make it! What's happened to you man! You look fantastic!!!' he says, sounding almost charitable with the flattering remark. It's Veer. Still small framed, he hasn't grown since the time I'd last seen him when he was 17.

'Thanks (!) Wish I could say the same about you (!)' I say as I free my hand from Steve's to hug Veer. Veer smells of expensive after-shave and alcohol. 'Silence from a man who has a snide remark for every touched nerve, you are losing your touch Mr Shroff!' I am surprised at Veer's subdued character.

'I didn't have you around to help me get creative with witty repartees...I've missed you.' Veer kisses me on my cheek and whispers into my ears 'Who is the mystery man?'

'Apologies...this is Steve. Steve and I work together in San Jose. Steve, Veer.' I say nervously. Steve looks down at Veer and smiles stretching out his extensive arm.

'Hey, nice to meet you 'mite',' I cringe. Veer's new lingo is an amalgamation of American and Australian slang. He shakes Steve's hand a little too enthusiastically. Veer appears uncomfortable standing close to Steve's towering body and loses no time to organise the seating arrangements.

'Do you guys want to sit by the bar or shall we grab a table here?' I begin to visualise a scene from the future where I am struggling to perch myself on an unstable bar stool and topple, head down first, wearing my dress over my face.

'This should suit us just fine,' I say, quickly lunging to a safe corner sofa with a table and three chairs.

'So, what can I get you both?' Veer asks rubbing his dark hands. He is wearing a faded pair of denim jeans and long mock sleeved pale blue and white T-shirt. Veer appears reluctant to let go of his teenage years, his small frame could still get away dressing twenty years too young but his face deceives him; his eyes which were his best features, are bloodshot and have sunken into the deep hollows of their sockets. Tiny pouches under his eyes give away tell tale signs of one too many late nights and heavy drinking.

'I'll just have something soft since the driver would need to be dropped off home. I don't think he'll find transport to head home given the weather conditions,' I say, feeling responsible for the poor man's plight.

'Bourbon on rocks for me, thank you.' Steve says, still bearing a smile and settling on a chair next to me. He helps himself to a few paper napkins on the table to dry his wet arms and face. He cleans the glass shell of his watch and taps on it to reassure that it's in working condition. He scrunches the paper napkins into a ball and tosses it into an ash tray.

Veer brings in our drinks and slides next to me on the sofa. He assesses me blatantly as he speaks.

'Tina tells me Rakesh and you have a son who is eleven years old!' He looks at Steve and says, 'This seems so surreal, I am meeting her after years and yet it doesn't seem that long. Does that make any sense to you?'

Steve nods violently before Veer volunteers to divulge a structured explanation. Steve and I exchange puzzled looks when Veer finishes his fifth 'single malt scotch' as we have barely taken a sip of ours. Veer checks his blackberry with one hand and his mobile messages with the other; whilst he orders drinks for himself as he keeps us suitably engaged about his life on the fast lane. After every drink Veer inches closer towards me until his thigh eventually touches mine. I am flushed and my throat feels dry. I take a gulp of my ice cold lemonade but it fails to bring down the temperature or soothe the dryness in my throat. I glance at Steve and wonder if he has noticed my unsteady nerves and Veer's stealthy progression. Steve seems distant; he is looking down at his drink with silent concentration. He runs his index finger unhurriedly around the rim of his glass. I begin to wonder if he is regretting making this trip to Mumbai with me. I haven't been of much company and I am now carting him around to meet my scotch loving friend through blustering weather.

Steve catches me looking at him. He forces a smile on his face as if to say he'd much rather be home. Steve excuses himself to visit the mens. He strides lazily across the room and stops by the bar to inspect Indian made spirits. Three bar tenders tussle and scurry towards Steve from different directions, to serve their white punter. I watch Steve bob his head wisely at the bar tenders who have obligingly lined up rows of bottles of spirits in every size, shape, form and colour, on the bar counter to enlighten the enquiring American mind.

'So what's the story with the American?' Veer asks as he drains his glass;I have lost count of the multiple 'single malts' he has consumed. His eyes flutter between Steve and my face.

'What story?' I know exactly what he means.

'You and him holding hands as you came in. You, travelling sans your husband. If memory serves me right, Rakesh was extremely possessive. He wouldn't let you out of his sight. Everything okay with you two?' Veer reads my transparent face, hungry for some scoop on my marital story.

'Every marriage goes through rough times, ours is no different,' I regret saying the words immediately. This is probably all Veer needed to know.

'Yes! I knew you'd married the wrong guy!' He sits up widening his ruby red eyes. 'I am so glad we met. Believe me when I say this, I was in love with you back then. It hurt when you rejected me which was why I left without a goodbye,' he whispers into my ears drenching me with whiskey fumes. 'I am sorry Nats, I do think things would have been different, had I stayed and wooed you till you'd said yes. You would have kept me grounded. Just look at me Nats….I have the world at my feet but there is still this huge void in my life. Tina would have mentioned this to you, I am divorced. I married my ex-wife only because she reminded me of you,' he looks at me intently, hesitates momentarily and then tenderly strokes my hair with the back of his fingers. His fingers slide down my bare arm and reach my right knee. He strokes it gently and watches me splutter on my drink bemused.

'Stop it, Veer! What do you think you are doing? I am a married woman and you have crossed your limits!' I whisper sternly, detaching his hand from my knee. I begin to tremble.

'If I know you well enough Nats, I would say, you were enjoying it. I can scorch you with my eyes Nats, imagine what my hands could do to you?' Veer declares cockily. I marvel at Veer's audacity to flirt and his alarming frequency to finish his drinks. He has probably consumed an entire bottle of whisky but he didn't seem drunk. His speech didn't slur and he hasn't thrown up yet.

'What's wrong with you? I am not one of your floozies so don't you pull that stunt on me again!' I hit his thigh with my clutch bag continually under the table. 'This was a bad idea. This whole episode has tarnished the memories of our friendship. I am leaving as soon as Steve gets back.' I announce moving away from him. I find myself sitting with one bum cheek suspended in air and the other on the edge of the sofa.

'Hey…Nats. I am sorry. I didn't mean to upset you,' he attempts to close in again, I wave my clutch bag at him and he immediately backs off. 'You have meant and mean so much to me. Of course I don't want to spoil what we've had. I guess I am just thrilled to see you again and realise that I am still insanely in love with you,' he says with his eyes fixed into mine. He looks regretful almost like a child who has just been told off.

A lone middle-aged man sat at the adjoining table blows smoke rings creating a cunning veneer for his eavesdropping activity. Another avid private conversation snoop! He shakes his head to indicate ambiguity in the declaration.

Steve joins us at the table with a freebie drink. He holds his drink up at the bar tenders to demonstrate his appreciation. The bar tenders stand next to each other and wave their table cloths at Steve like cheerleaders waving their pompoms. He turns to look at me to give me an update on his generous new buddies. His enthusiasm fades away quickly when I show no interest as I am finding it increasingly hard to look comfortable sitting on thin air and fighting off a friend-turned-sensualist. I begin to fabricate a logical excuse to escape Veer's unanticipated overtures. Although the experience of being touched by Veers crafty fingers was mildly pleasurable, I am trying to make sense of it all. Veer plays it cool and prepares to fetch another drink for himself.

'Veer, I think we must call it a night now, Steve isn't feeling too well,' I say, looking sympathetically at Steve who was looking forward to enjoying his complimentary drink.

'I am not?' Steve is confused and shocked to find his body talking to me. I glare at Steve and he immediately begins to rub his belly 'Oh yeah! That food at your sister's is still alive in here, therefore the long trip to the loo.'

'That's' very kind of you to share that piece of information with us, Steve!' I turn to Veer who has begun to look cagey. 'Veer, it was good to see you again,' I say, getting up from the edge of the sofa.

'The 'pleasure' was all mine,' Veer caresses his stubble with the same hand that stroked my knee moments ago. 'So are we meeting Priti tomorrow?' he asks, tucking his Blackberry and his mobile into his side pockets. He is steady as a rock while I am legless, trembling after one lemonade and an intimate encounter with Veer.

'I think it's best if I meet her on my own,' I feel nauseous as his intentions to meet Priti don't appear genuine.

'Don't leave the country without a 'goodbye' Nats,' Veer appears hurt with the sudden change in plans. He hugs me briefly and kisses me softly on the corner of my mouth, grazing my skin with his coarse stubble. 'I am still in love with you, we've wasted too many years. And time my sweets, is luxury,' Veer whispers causing me to have a brief paralytic attack.

The grateful driver is given a lift to his home. I take control of the wheels, fortunately the weather has calmed down, shame I couldn't say the same about my nerves. Steve gets me to pull over to one side after we've travelled a short distance. I begin to wonder if he was being truthful about his indigestion after all.

'I know it's none of my business but is there something brewing between Veer and you? I could sense some serious undercurrents back there,' Steve says.

'Don't be ridiculous! But I'll be honest, he did try coming on to me when you'd disappeared. Where were you when I needed protecting? I am not happy with your services,' I joke, disguising my confusion, still unsure if I found the intimacy with Veer pleasurable or distasteful. Rakesh had never shown recklessness of this nature. Is Veer genuinely in love with me or was I sending out wrong signals? Did Veer think I was 'available' when he saw me holding Steve's hand?

The 'hand' in question was resting behind me on my seat's head rest and has now travelled to the nape of my neck. A finger traces the outline of my face and stops on my lips. Steve leans towards me, his eyes and finger resting on my quivering lips. The streetlights shine on him and I see three top buttons of his shirt are undone exposing his broad muscular chest. My heart is thumping so loud that I am afraid Steve might hear it. My fingers tighten around the steering wheel as his lips are about to touch mine.

'You look incredibly delicious Tash and I want to devour you this instant, just tell me it's over between you and the doctor,' Steve says, filled with Dutch courage and drunken hope.

Chapter Eighteen

Sitting on a creaking concave cane swing in the patio, I mull over last night's events over a steaming cup of ginger tea. I contemplate Googling for some valuable advice on the internet but change my mind following a quick flashback. I recall a time when Rishab was distraught losing his Guinea pig when he found it lying on its back facing heavenwards, in its tiny glass house. When I politely turned down the request to lay the 'rodent' to rest, he threw a question at the world wide web hoping someone out there would have an answer to his 'fur ball' woes. 'Chuck it in the bin!' 'Flush it down the toilet!' 'Feed it to your cat!' left the grief stricken son traumatized for days.

In India you are seldom short of company even when you want to be left alone. I soon find myself encircled by members of the family who uncannily find an activity to pursue in and around the patio. Rishab wanders in with his battered Nintendo and sinks into a cushioned cane chair, propping his legs up comfortably. His Martian enemies get his unswerving attention as he launches missiles by merely pressing two buttons. A band comprising of a trumpet player and drummer, play a piercing tune to declare victory each time an unsuspecting defenceless Martian is destroyed. A menacing Rishab is ecstatic with the results.

Mrs Roy sashays in wearing a designer sari, carrying an aubergine plastic watering can; that could barely hold 500 ml fluid in it. Mrs Roy enjoys showing the world that despite having maids who are happy to hold her saucer whilst she slurps her Darjeeling tea daintily from a porcelain cup; she is quite content to do some of the housework herself. She waters a 10-foot tall potted rubber plant with eight drops of water and then swishes to the next pot. If it wasn't for our maid these plants would have been replaced by the plastic variety.

Mother catches sight of our neighbour Mrs Desai, who has a penchant for society gossip. Through exuberant eyes and hand movements they communicate about Mrs Shah's twenty-one year old son having an affair with a forty year old Mrs Vaswani who incidentally lives on the floor below us. Mrs Desai has an eagle's view from her flat into naughty Mrs Vaswani's flat whose shenanigans haven't gone unnoticed. They then move on to young Simi, a television actress who moved to the city from a small town - Chandigarh. Mrs Desai has spotted Simi's unsavoury looking lads on various occasions entering her flat and leaving at wee hours of the morning. It makes me wonder if Mrs Desai has all this information stored in a password protected worklog 'spread'sheet in her husband's computer.

'I will bring this up in the next meeting! We have young impressionable children living here, what will people say? *Cheee!*' She looks aghast. She suddenly notices my presence, her grimacing face fakes a smile. 'Hello Natasha. When are you having your second child? How is America?' I wonder how I should interpret the random questions and reply graciously. Fortunately Mrs Desai is just making polite conversation and focuses her attention on Mrs Roy again. 'Our apartment prices will fall, if word gets out!' she thunders.

Mr Roy strolls in with this morning's *Economic Times* tucked under his arms. He is wearing a pale green Ralph Lauren shirt on black cotton shorts. A black leather belt is strapped on in an attempt to turn the casual ensemble to smart-casual. Tina and I have screeched ourselves hoarse voicing our opposition and concerns on this look. He kisses me on my head and gives a trendy 'Hi Five' to Rishab who responds without moving his eyes from his gadget's screen. Mr Roy slumps into the living room sofa and unfolds the newspaper noisily in a premeditated effort to disrupt Mrs Roy's tittle-tattle. His face breaks into a mischievous smile when Mrs Roy isn't best pleased. Soon the smile leaks away as his breakfast makes a grand entrance on a carved wooden trolley pushed by our maid, Hema. Mr Roy looks at the unpalatable spread tutting and shaking his head. Ever since his health scare, his meals are prepared under mother's strict supervision. Today's breakfast comprises of one poached egg on a dried Rye toast, two halves of peaches, one pot of very weak sugarless tea and bountiful of multicoloured medications.

'Prisoners are better fed!' he says with a look that is required to generate compassion.

'Did you and Steve have a good night out? What time did you get back?' *Pa* questions taking a bite of the Rye toast and swallows it like a medicated pill with large sips of tea. The fatherly interrogation will continue till I am aged 100.

'*Pa*! I am not a child anymore…if you really want to know we did get back at two. Steve was starving and all the restaurants were shut. Finally fed him some street food and he absolutely loved it!' Mr Roy has begun dribbling. 'Look *Pa*, I'd really love to stay and chat about the Shammi kebabs you can't have in this lifetime…but I've got to have a shower before Rishab gets in there and turns it into a war zone. I am meeting Priti in a few minutes.'

'You have become cruel like your mother. I can't enjoy good food and now I can't talk about it either!' *Pa* throws a small piece of Rye toast on a plate dramatically and then picks it up again to swallow it with his tea. 'What about Steve?' Mr Roy is hoping for another male bonding session.

'Tina's taking him sightseeing and I think there is a little visit to the office planned in the itinerary,' I say.

A few minutes later, I find myself ringing a doorbell. Priti's mum answers the door. The figure standing in front of me is no more a plump bubbly figure. Three full bodied individuals seemed to have left the large frame. If it wasn't the clearly identifiable smile it would have been hard to recognise her. Her thick black mane has turned into straggly bits of grey hair. Priti's mum was known for her love for gold jewellery and expensive clothes. However, today I find her in shabby, unkempt attire.

'Natasha! So good to see you *beti*. Come in, Priti will be so pleased to see you.' There is a hint of sadness in her smile.

I impulsively hug her tight, I can sense she is unhappy and I want to make it all evaporate. My eyes moisten as Priti's mum dissolves into my arms.

We compose ourselves as she leads me to Priti's room. I quickly become aware of the condition of the stately home, the grandeur long gone. Naked light bulbs substitute crystal chandeliers, dilapidated walls yearn a lick of fresh paint, a few pieces of old furniture that are haphazardly arranged have dirt and sweat marks over them.

I know my way to Priti's room, however, I doubt myself as I fail to get the same vibe I got years ago. I enter a dark room and Priti's mum walks past me to draw the curtains. My heart sinks, I find Priti sitting upright on her bed in complete darkness. Dust and medicated syrup bottles adorn the side table.

'Natasha!' Priti says quietly as she holds up her arms for a hug. She makes no attempt to get out of bed.

'Gosh! Priti!' I scream and make a dash towards Priti and throw myself on her. The bed groans and creates a crater to accommodate my body.

'I'll leave you two alone….can I get you something?' Priti's mum asks, half smiling and half blinking away her tears.

'No thank you, aunty, I've just had to gulp down Rishab's soggy breakfast cereal all because he is too busy playing with his gadgets. When I tried yelling, I was ticked off by my own parents for being too harsh on their grandson!' I say, shaking my head. She smiles and walks away quietly.

I turn around to look at Priti. She looks older than I'd imagined. Wearing no make-up and dressed in a garment that very closely resembled a sack, she looks down shamefaced unable to look me in the eye. Tears roll down silently.

'Why?' I ask a monosyllabic question loaded with hidden connotations. I get more tears.

'Come on, you've got to talk to someone. You'll make yourself ill… Priti, for God's sake at least think of your little girl. Talk to me babes….!' I urge unable to fight back my own tears.

Priti breaks down in my arms, holding me and crying inconsolably. I stroke her hair and hold her close. Why was she hurting so much? What could this sensitive, loving soul have done so wrong that she felt it was necessary to punish herself in this twisted way?

Priti begins to free herself from years of solely carrying the hurt, anguish and pain she suffered at the hands of Deepak. I cannot come to terms with the reality as I had painted a pretty picture of a well natured, subdued, kind-hearted Deepak.

The first few weeks of their marriage were bliss, but soon there were demands for *dowry* made by Deepak. Dowry, though illegal is still prevalent in this rapidly changing society in India.

In the ancient Hindu customs the term '*Dowry*' was derived from the word '*Kanyadan*' which signifies the brides family gifting the groom with money, or any other demands made by him or his greedy family. If the demands are not met, the groom and his family decide to tackle the problem by making life a living hell for the victim. Sometimes the ill-treatment can go beyond physical violence and can end in horrific circumstances. Bride-burning is common in even in urban cities. The perfectly healthy unsuspecting victim is doused in cooking oil and lit alive. Since divorce is still taboo, it is not always looked upon as an alternative in conservative families.

When Deepak's business venture went belly up, he applied pressure tactics on Priti to demand money from her father. When she refused, he turned to violence, the abuses were initially verbal which soon turned physical. The 'kind hands' that helped her make the most significant decision of her life; were now raised to brutally assault her. The violence escalated after the birth of her daughter - Ria. Deepak's sisters and parents took turns in hurling abuses and casting doubts on Priti's pristine character. Deepak made sure Priti had no relatives, friends or life of her own. He spent a disproportionate amount of time demeaning Priti. On many occasions he would come home drunk as a skunk and urinate on Priti, spit on her face, pull chunks of hair, kick and punch her to release his stress. Maybe going to the gym was not an option. Why pay money when you can have a workout for free!

There were times when Deepak would sneak into her room and record her sobbing. The mentalist perceived this would gain him a 'good standing certificate' from the judge in case Priti decided to drag him to court. He would then whip out his evidence to prove Priti suffered from depression and was making up random stories to tarnish his well preserved reputation. Priti once found images of Deepak with self inflicted wounds all stashed away nicely for a rainy day.

Deepak gained complete control over Priti by alienating her from her friends and family. She wasn't allowed to even stay in contact with her parents. Itemised phone billings were checked and saved history on the home computer were monitored on a daily basis. Gradually Priti began to withdraw more and more into her shell unable to challenge her husband on her own.

Meanwhile, Neeraj, Priti's brother made a fine mess of things when he lost the family fortune on drugs, alcohol and women. He died a couple of years ago of drug overdose. Priti's aging father unable to bear the grief of losing the business, his son's untimely death and his daughter's ill treatment, suffered a breakdown. He has been a recluse since.

Bundling Ria into a taxi, Priti managed to conjure up enough courage to escape Deepak's clutches and headed straight to her parents' house.

One fine Sunday morning Priti dropped Ria to her friend's house and returned home only to swallow umpteen pain killers as casually as one would take vitamin supplements. Priti had locked the door and instructed her mother not to disturb her faking a throbbing headache. Priti was discovered unconscious by her mother who came knocking on the door to remind her to pick Ria up from her friend's house.

Deepak was informed of the incident and showed a bit of humility by visiting her at the hospital. Although Deepak's second visit resulted in seven emaciated ward boys escorting him out of the hospital premises. Priti's brave mother was keen to press charges. However, Priti wouldn't allow this to happen as he was after all the father of their child and he has been a good father if not a role model to her. I wonder if one can be a good father and a bad role model.

'Surely you have heard of the word 'Divorce'?' I am annoyed at Priti's thoughtless actions. 'Killing yourself isn't the answer.'

'My father didn't let me finish my education, who would employ me in this age of manufactured MBAs? I have no money to my name, I didn't want to burden my parents with my problems. I knew Deepak would look after Ria. I just felt all the doors shut on me Natasha. I just couldn't see a way out of this mess. Besides, Deepak refused to give me a divorce. My coping resources exceeded the pain I was enduring...' she dithers

'That's crap! Did you even stop to think of Ria? Did you seriously think Deepak would instil values and morals into her? You just found an easy way out of your problem. And what about your mum, eh? Isn't it her time to be looked after? Instead you would have left her with more responsibilities...You could have called me or Tina...Tina could have helped you find a job. Why didn't you call me, Priti? Why did you shut me out?' We cry until our tears run dry and I have no more pocket tissues left in my handbag.

'Listen, to me. You've done all your crying. That animal who masquerades as a human being doesn't deserve your tears. You've got to be brave, for your parents, Ria and most importantly for yourself. Step one would be divorce on the grounds of behaviour, if he swells his chest and starts drumming it, he has got my father and brother-in-law to answer to. The reason why Deepak has got away for so many years doing what he did is because you don't have anyone to stand up to him in your family. Step two would be to make you independent and that's a piece of cake as Tina's looking for reliable staff all the time and knowing the person you are, you will fit in like a glove in the glam world...although we'll need to get you out of that sack first!!!' I say sounding serious.

'Natasha - the fashion police! I never thought I would 'live' to see this day!' Priti says and we laugh uproariously.

Chapter Nineteen

'Are you sure you want to do this on your own?' I ask Steve as we watch Sunil load the airport trolley a little too eagerly, anticipating a generous tip for his efforts.

It has been awkward since Steve's unpredictable drunken move on me. We had been making feeble excuses to avoid each other. Steve, over the past few days had been touring the city, this time preferring to be ably guided by Tina.

Seven street urchins have formed a circular ring around Steve; each tugging different ends of his shirt. Tina has toughened this American cookie; he pays no attention to the septuplets' demands and speaks to me as though he is completely unaware of their existence.

'Yeah, I'll be fine. Besides Tina has made all the arrangements, I am sure I'll be well looked after,' Steve had made an impetuous decision to continue his expedition across India on his own and head back to the US thereafter.

'I feel terrible abandoning you like this.'

'You are not!' Determined to establish eye contact the persevering imps' tugs get forceful, lowering Steve's immense figure. 'SCCRRRRAAAAAM!!!' Steve finally cracks unable to bear the intrusion into his personal space. The septuplet retreat, their eyes bulging in shock, they disperse at the same lightening speed they had once appeared to orbit around their American prey. 'I never really got to tell you this…' he quickly composes himself 'I think we've got something special between us. We've know each other for a while…now. I like you kid, but I reckon you are holding back. I know you are still attached and the rest of it... but I can't help how I feel about you. I'll let you sort that pretty little head while I am gone,' He lowers his body and deposits a light kiss near my mouth. Sunil stunned by the unexpected blatant display of affections has fallen into the boot of the car still holding Steve's rug sack in his hand.

I am driven home with a sense of emptiness, why did our goodbyes seems so final? Just then I receive a text from Veer – *'I am going out of my mind thinking about u. Meet me - Sejoh's @ 7'* I had been ignoring Veer's flirtatious text messages since the time I'd met him at Lou's Blues; each one taking me closer to the tempting path of adultery. I surprise myself by giving in to his outrageously cheesy message.

I surprise myself even further attempting to stage another high-five-worthy winsome entry, by wearing a nude pink pencil skirt and teaming it with a pair of killer heels and white cowl neck silk top. I allow myself to experience the feeling of excitement of going out on a first date.

I trot into the urban uber-chic bar/restaurant beaming with uncontrollable buzz. I catch sight of Veer lounging on a rust orange Barcelona settee. The five empty glasses on the table indicate Veer's evening had begun much before my arrival. He winks at me to indicate that he has recognised me. He instructs me to sit by lightly beating the space next to him but I am unable to move as my heel is wedged between two wooden floorboards. I have to act fast and furious. I pretend to have forgotten something and rummage through my clutch bag, a crafty distraction while I grunt softly as I make a discreet monumental effort to free my trapped heel.

Two waiters who see through my façade hold my unsteady body while another frees the jammed heel. I suspect they have rescued many inexpert trotters who've fallen prey to these notorious floorboards. I catch sight of a small cluster of twenty-somethings elbowing each other and sniggering overtly.

'Like I'd mentioned earlier you've not changed!' Veer smiles broadly revealing his small teeth. He holds my hand firmly and seats me at the exact spot he'd reserved to accommodate my bottom. 'I think I'll skip the meal and ravish you instead...' he whispers into my ears. Thick dark hair is in display on the back of his hands, what Veer lacks on his crown has ample and more neck downwards. I marvel at the degree of effort required to sprout and maintain the five o'clock stubble.

'Have you had company?' I ask, pointing at the empty glasses on the table, cleverly digressing Veer's attention and disguising my weakened nerves.

'Are you implying I drink too much?' Veer straightens up taking offence to my oral observation. 'FYI, I am the fittest I have ever been.' *Oh dear! Here we go again!* I had forgotten just how much in love Veer was with himself. Instantly, I regret the clever sarcasm. I hold back the urge to disagree and wonder if he has ever taken notice of the small soft belly resting over his knees. 'Men my age wouldn't dream of competing in the marathons I've participated in. It's all down to discipline...a balanced diet of pomegranate juice, kebabs and scotch.'

'Fascinating (!) Aren't you full of surprises!' I fake a look of sheer disbelief.

'That's not very nice. I am so good to you and what do I get in return? Shot down by more insults and sarcasms,' Veer appears wounded, upper lip sucked in and lower lip rolled out; his advances taking on a new element, an approach to generate sympathy.

A waiter has been briefed on his punters 'balanced diet', a drink appears steadfast, keeping up with the same rate as an empty scotch glass is placed on the table we are sat at. I throw caution to the wind and order a glass of white wine.

'Hey, have you kept in touch with Diya and Sanjay?' I demand a quick update on the inseparable duo.

Veer knocks back another drink like it's a small portion of his RDA. Veer's RDA interpretation would probably read 'Recommended Daily Alcohol-intake'. He checks his surgically attached Blackberry and mobile phone possibly to read on newsletter updates on Diya and Sanjay.

Sanjay and Diya, as Veer tells me, were married soon after completing their Chartered Accountancy. They were so in tune with each other, their aspirations were frighteningly similar. Diya, the smarter one of the two, set up her own firm roping in super affluent clients smoothly in the process. Sanjay unable to deal with his wife's success decided his ego was far more precious than his wife's soaring career. Diya's success was penalised and was rewarded with a quick divorce. Sanjay now works for an Indian jeweller in Dubai. Sanjay is in the city visiting his family but it's been a while since Veer has heard from Diya.

Veer has ordered his special beetroot and lemongrass salad, a dish concocted as per Veer's instructions to assist in neutralizing the damaging effects of alcohol; but to me it looked like autopsy on a plate.

A horizontally-challenged middle aged man and a pretty young girl are sat next to our table. I had assumed they were father and daughter until I find the sleazy ugly mug stroking her neck in an un-fatherly fashion. The girl appears to enjoy the attention and starts sucking one of stubs attached to the stroking hand.

There is a distinct class difference in India. To enjoy the pleasures of high life and an effort to 'keep up with the Jones'', young women and men from less fortunate background are turning to a lucrative profession of playing 'escorts' to rich codgers.

I begin to remind myself of the Indian scriptures that speak about respecting women. But has this been forgotten in urban India? Sanjay's insecurities and status obviously seems to have topped his list of priorities, Deepak, releasing his anger and fury out on a defenceless wife, rich old foggies buying sex and love from the less fortunate who are young enough to be their grandchildren.

Am I being too judgemental? I speak about loose morals and integrity but I find myself sat in a bar igniting passion in Veer who appears to have this quality in abundance. I set the mental record straight. I am allowed to feel desired, besides; Rakesh and I are on trial separation. I need to test the unexplored hidden depths of this unfamiliar territory. I feel young and strangely womanly again.

My stomach tightens as I find Veers fingers entwine mine. The

Blackberry seems to have switched hands. It's big of the other hand to charitably accommodate both the gadgets. I sense a soft kiss on my bare arm, my stomach now a size of a tiny pea. My first instinct is to scan the room if this explicit illustration of affection has an audience, oddly everyone in the room are engaged in similar recreation.

I find Veer studying my face, his eyes finally resting on my quivering lips. I guzzle down my wine like its sparkling mineral water, this time not remembering to swirl, sniff and spurt it in my mouth.

'Veer, I really don't think this is a good idea! I am married and I suppose you have a girlfriend?'

'Easy baby…we are just enjoying the evening. No harm done,' Veer seems to be in control of the situation and I could tell he has had ample performances of this nature.

'You haven't answered my question…do you have a girlfriend?' I want to know the truth and nothing but the truth without sounding incredibly jealous.

'The green eyed monster has reared its ugly head….you look so sexy when you are jealous,' Veer has definitely Googled for cheesy one liners.

'Well?' *You are not getting away so easily mister.*

'Yes…but it's nothing serious. In fact we are heading for splitville soon. She has been getting up my wick lately,' he says gravely.

'Does she have a name?'

'Nazia!'

'Muslim?'

'Yup,' Veer murmurs gloomily.

'Wow (!) You don't do things by halves, do you?' Veer is more daring than I'd thought. He's barely divorced and now involved in an interfaith relationship. He may have been axed from the family tree with one mighty blow by now. 'How long have you been seeing her?'

Veer does some number crunching with his fingers, looks thoughtful and comes up with a figure 'Four years!'

'And you say it's not serious?' *I am not buying 'I think we are not compatible' crap.*

'Well it was at first, but now I am not so sure. We have been falling out quite often lately. I've been getting grief from my family because of her religion.' *Didn't you see that coming?* 'And now I don't think it's worth it. She can get insanely insecure. I have to constantly update her on my whereabouts,' which now explained the surgically attached appendages, 'it can get a bit claustrophobic for a free spirit like me.'

'You don't say (!)'

Chapter Twenty

Tina decides to treat me to a brunch in Olive, a perennially casual-chic restaurant that serves scrumptious Mediterranean food. The white walls with whiter furnishings eatery scream 'GREECE!'

'Let's all have a night out! Let's go clubbing!' Tina declares brightly. Tina probably realises I need cheering. There is a certain feeling of discontent and emptiness with Steve's departure and Priti's horrific suffering. It is a mixed bag of emotions as my thoughts also encompass Veer. On one hand his attention did bring me a bit of joy; on the other I couldn't quite make of his intentions. I couldn't help but get the feeling that I was watching lives and personalities evolve before my very eyes. I have been away from India too long. This is the same city, country, I grew up in. The same people I have known for decades, yet I fail to comprehend how life and circumstances have changed some so dramatically.

On the other hand, it fills me with pride to see India embracing modernisation so positively, boundaries between communities are diminishing; the economy is getting stronger than ever; limitless avenues are now open to the young and talented. For me, there has always been a sense of belonging.

'Actually, hang on a minute...' Tina appears to have a better idea and recoils from her own ingenious, 'Why not have a reunion of some sort? It seems ages since I've hooked up with my old friends. You try to persuade Priti and whoever else you'd like to touch base with and I'll contact some of my old mates?' Apart from me I fail to recollect who Tina hung out with. Tina whips out her contacts book from her Prada handbag and noisily flicks through pages. She runs down her fingers through all the alphabetically listed names. Her bright smile fades away quickly as she turns the pages. She glances at her iPhone and her spirits leap once again. She punches the touch screen with her pink varnished thumb nail frantically. She looks up at me disheartened. Just as I thought!

'You could try Facebook?' I suggest and am immediately rewarded with a look of horror.

'I do NOT need the cyber world to network!' she says firmly. 'Anyway it's full of narcissistic losers uploading flattering holiday and social pictures of themselves.'

'You do have a point,' I nod in complete agreement. There was nothing of any value said or done on these social networking sites. The other day I read a post that said 'Having a cuppa...' *Huh? What am I going to do with that information?'*

Rishab and I did go through a period when we were practically living in the cyber world, diligently following updates and feeds on Twitter and Facebook. Until one morning I made a life changing decision to deactivate our various virtual accounts and renounce the cyber world and embrace the real world to reconnect and establish eye contact with 'the son'. Rishab failed to find any meaning to my bizarre act of randomness and found solace in his Nintendo! Which reminded me the Nintendo will be next to bite the dust. It's always important to introduce changes gradually.

'Hey...wait a minute...let's invite Kunal Khanna!' Tina squeals loud and hysterical.

'Kunal Khanna? Not 'The Kunal Khanna' from our college?' I screech with excitement. Tina nods mutely wearing the biggest smile on her face, proud to have now established, she did have friends in college and that she's even managed to stay in contact with one of them.

'When did you get in touch with him?' I feel compelled to ask before I comfortably slip into reminiscing my days in college. I dreamily recollect my occasional sightings of this gorgeous creature. Kunal Khanna was the demi-god in our college. It seems funny to repeatedly attach his last name to his first name. But that's how it was even back then. He was not any Kunal, he was 'Kunal Khanna'. The one and only. Over six foot tall, broad shouldered and face to die for. Freshly imported from America, the USP of this durable product was his accent. His family lived in America for major part of his childhood running a family owned jewellery shop. Unfortunately his father was robbed and gunned down by burly men in balaclavas. The stash was never recovered and the men went AWOL with the booty.

Having no means of support or income and being originally from Mumbai, his mother decided to move back to the city with Kunal and his two sisters.

Kunal was Tina's batch mate and I was a little saddened to see him leave our college when he graduated with Tina. Tina and I (like the zillion other girls in college) had nursed a secret crush on him.

'He is a friend of Ricky's now. We got to know of him through work,' Tina explains. 'He has set up this hugely successful online recruitment firm and obviously has a lot of staff working under him. We had assisted in organising a team building 'away day' for his workforce. I immediately recognised him from college when he'd walked into our office to meet Ricky.

With that information I deduce he cannot be classified as an old friend from college but surely it will be a shame to deny him entry into this 'reunion of some sort'.

'Tell me more...is he married?' I slobber for more information.

'Yeah...she is so odd...you've got to meet her...we'll have a right laugh!' Tina promises. 'In fact I find them both quite odd. They have this strange obsession to co-ordinate clothes!' Tina fears a lot of couples in their thirties cling on to their youth and develop odd tendencies in the process. 'But Ricky seems to get on with him and I must admit he is well connected and has given us some good accounts,' Tina admits grudgingly.

'By the way...have you sorted things out with Rakesh?' Tina asks tentatively, suddenly looking serious.

'Tina...I don't know...I know it's not fair on him...but I am not so sure about going back to him,' although it seems like it's a shame to bring up the subject of my failing marriage in a stunning ambience like the one we are in, I experience a feeling of relief that I am finally being able to open up to Tina. 'We don't seem to connect like a couple any more...we don't have a partnership of any kind...isn't that what marriage is about? We've stopped doing things as a family. His patients are his number one priority and Rishab and I barely make it to the Top 100 on his list of priorities (!)' I let out a deep sigh expelling my hidden anguish.

'Surely, you don't mean that! Rakesh worships you and Rishab is his world...anyone can see that,' Tina tries her best to lift the imaginary blinkers. I wonder if we were talking about the same person. Somehow the words 'worship' and 'adore' don't sit well with Rakesh anymore. Yes, he would have loved me enough to go against the wishes of 'mummy dearest' but lately I haven't seen Rakesh ever displaying any form of emotions other than concerns for his loopy patients. Why do I keep referring to his patients in a derogatory manner? When did I get so bitter and twisted?

'Look Natasha, we have all got to compromise when it comes to marriage. I accepted Ricky for who he is and he's done the same. There are times when I've thought maybe it's not working. Our marriage is no different we've had our ups and down. But we've managed to work through them.'

'Could you elaborate on the downs?' I can sense all is not right in the marital paradise.

Tina shocks me with a bit of suppressed history. With reluctance she relates an incident when she had switched on Ricky's laptop to access information on Mr Bhimani, whose daughter's lavish wedding they'd organised.

Only Tina, didn't have much 'switching on' to do. Ricky had naively left his Facebook account logged on and for all to access, accidently! She would otherwise have logged off for him obliging only if there weren't a pair of boobs staring back at her giving her the come on! On further investigation she unearthed series of faceless but bountiful and boobieful photographs uploaded for Ricky's private viewings. The perky assets belonged to a young recruit who had recently joined our Bangalore division as an Apprentice.

Young girls today are so blinded by success that some are willing to go to great lengths to compromise. Who can blame them? We are after all the second largest populated country in the world. The fight for survival is fierce.

Ricky regrettably came clean about his virtual fascination. As Tina found out, he wasn't working as hard to pitch the high profile 'Precision' – a corporate account, as he'd led her to believe. Ricky being a man in his early forties was flattered by the attention from a young woman. It was perfectly innocent; he encouraged the cyber exhibits but at the same time didn't cave in to temptation as he had too much to lose. Smart man!

I quickly grasp the 'social networking site aversion' factor.

After the disciplinary hearing, Miss Twin Peaks was given her marching orders and candidly informed not to live in hope of a glowing reference. Lessons were learnt. Standards were set. And honour and harmony was rapidly restored with the Apprentice's dishonourable exit.

Wow! So much had happened in my own family and I seem to learn something new every day.

'So who are you going to invite?' Tina asks curiously just as our orders are placed on the table. Tina clearly put the past behind her and let the dust settle. She is stronger and more forgiving than I'd thought.

'Priti, Veer...and I might ask Veer to get Sanjay along to join us. What do you think?' I ask, tearing and dunking a piece of warm pita bread in moreishly nutty hummus drizzled with rich olive oil.

'Ppppfff! 'Hardly a merry bunch!' she spits out her Falafel. It takes a lot for our Tina to forget her etiquette and with that I realise Veer must have strong undesirable effects on her. 'What do you want me to say? I don't like Veer and like Sanjay even less; in fact I don't know Sanjay at all.'

'It's just one night. It'll be interesting to find out what he's been up to. Besides if we are thinking of going clubbing we need someone to pair up Priti with. 'Stags' can't gain entry in most places. '

'I'd rather eat my own eyeballs...sorry they just don't do it for me,' Tina shakes her head miserably. I agree. It is way too early to take Priti anywhere social, never mind clubbing.

'Bwwwaaaa haaa haaa!!' we hear loud raucous laughter behind us. I jump with fright and my head jerks around to catch sight of a group of women ranging between the age of 25 and 80 decked in brightest evening clothes, adorning tons of make-up and jewellery.

Judging by the inappropriate dress code and war paint of the merrymakers - a kitty party in process I conclude.

Being out of the Indian 'kitty' social circuit in the States as my 'working' status disqualified my admission, I haven't seen these congregations for a while. Kitty parties of late have become the quintessential social jaunt for bored housewives flushed with money. The bars have been set higher as the dynamics of these glamorised girly leisure meetings have changed over the years. The venues which were originally in the comfort of the host's humble home have now shift to trendy bars and restaurants. The chosen venues usually reflect upon on the spending capacity and profile of the group.

Although the groups have upped their game in certain aspects, the content and dress codes have remained the same. The agenda of these high profile meetings often entails a range of activities. It usually kick starts with briefing the group on matters arising, when members bring the others up to speed with juicy gossip updates and ultimate shockers on relatives, friends, neighbours, etc (mothers-in-law usually top the hit list). The motor mouths replenish the lost calories with three-course meals and copious amount of drinking and smoking (some might steer clear from alcohol and nicotine, fearing disrepute and being spoken about at similar meetings hosted elsewhere). The gathering ends on a high when members pool in Rs 100 – Rs 20,000 (or more depending on the social status of the network). The winner of the kitty aka pool is imposed with the task of organising the next meeting. Minutes are never taken and that's the unwritten rule! What's said at the meeting stays between the respected members of the group lest they want to be evicted out of the network and be left without a life outside the four walls of their home.

Chapter Twenty One

I couldn't help reflecting on how Priti has been left to her own devices to pick up the pieces. Where is the society that condemns love marriages and pressured Priti's family to find a groom of their choice? Disturbing stories of 'honour killing' still arise in the so called educated middle-class urban society and is not confined to just the rural communities when couples decide to elope and get married against the parents' wishes. What right does the society have to dictate who you should or shouldn't spend the rest of your life with?

It's been an eventful two weeks. Priti had made a swift and speedy recovery from her domestic setback. She is more in control of her life than she had ever been. It is amazing how a little bit of support from family and friends can inject confidence in the weakest. Priti agreed to work-shadow Tina to get a flavour of the workings of an event management firm. Tina felt this would be a great starting point to gauge where Priti's interests lie. *Pa* and Ricky joined forces to put Priti in touch with one of most prominent family/divorce solicitors in the city – Mrs Pratibha Kulkarni. *Pa* generously offered to pay for her legal services.

It all became crystal clear why *Pa* called Mrs Kulkarni – 'a force to reckon with' when Priti and I met her for the first time. My initial impressions of Mrs Kulkarni didn't work in her favour. I wondered if *Pa* had secretly stopped taking his medications and got his legal teams mixed up. I expected a placid sympathetic solicitor who would rock Priti in her arms, assuring her of child support, hefty alimony and a possible lengthy prison sentence for Deepak and his greedy platoon.

But instead we were hurriedly pushed into a room by a peon who had some serious civility issues. You can measure the success of an individual in India by assessing the behaviour of their employees even those that are on the bottom rung! Judging by the black and white hair streaks, one could tell she has had years of experience chewing the opposition party and spitting them out like they were mouldy food. She appeared to be in her early sixties and at our first meeting, stared sternly at us like we were keeping her from her retirement. Her starched stiff stereotypical white and cream sari suggested she did not tolerate wimps. I shot one look at defeated Priti and knew I had my work cut out to establish good working relationships between the two.

The first few meetings with Mrs Kulkarni were painful for Priti as she had to relive and revisit the horrifying ordeal Deepak put her through; I wondered if we had taken a few steps back, as just as I was feeling hopeful of getting my old friend back, now I wasn't so sure.

The subsequent meetings that followed, I saw perceptible changes in Priti. I could now see how gender dynamics could bring massive changes by empowering women, freedom and financial security. Priti became more determined than ever to put her past behind her and look ahead to the future. The thought often crossed my mind if I was beginning to see a bit of Mrs Kulkarni in Priti, especially when she punched the air and hit Mrs Kulkarni's table with her fist every time Deepak's name was mentioned. Deepak's lame threats diminished as days went by especially when Ricky's sim card was cleverly swapped for Priti's. At Mrs Kulkarni's insistence Priti was being treated by a therapist. I wondered if I could have a few sessions myself to neutralise the effects after silently enduring double doses of Mrs Kulkarni. But on the other hand, I was on a high to see Priti's life taking shape, completely ignorant of the fact that mine was spiralling out of control!

'Hey sweetie...can I get2 c ur pretty face 2nite?' It's Veer's latest text message.

I am bubbling and my stomach feels taut with excitement, even though we have been seeing each other every other night since the time I met him at Sejoh's. Tina would be upset if she ever found out about the number of times Veer and I have hooked up. She means well, bless her. If she only knew Veer the way I did, she would think differently.

'Sure, *ver do u wanna meet?*' I reply. I was getting increasingly good with abbreviated texts.

'*Can you pick me up @7. I'll b stood outside my workplace.*'

As I approach Veer's office, I reduce the speed of my car in a deliberate attempt to scan the crowded streets for a familiar figure. Drivers blare their horns at me and don't hold back their words or vulgar gestures to show their anger for slowing them down as they zip by me. *Oh! I hate Veer for being so insignificant! Or did the mysterious Nazia impulsively decide to surprise her man and he has been unable to contact me!* Dread begins to slowly slide inside me, I get a sinking feeling this may well be true. I decide I hate her for being in Veer's life.

Just then, I spot what looked like Veer's young double, leaning against an old tree trunk, leisurely inhaling nicotine. Could it be Veer sporting a bandanna? Oh my God! Even Veer couldn't commit this fashion sacrilege! As if that isn't enough to alert the fashion police, Veer has his sunglasses on when the sun had set a couple of hours ago. I realise his vision doesn't seem impaired despite the dark shades. He recognises the car, flicks the cigarette which still has a few puffs left in it and takes slow lazy strides towards the car.

Veer clicks the seatbelt in place and strokes my cheek. Of late the cheek stroke has replaced the customary 'hello' greeting. 'Is this your evening ensemble? You do know you are bang on trend if you were twenty years younger and the sun was still shining (!) Do you realise you don't need those shades anymore? We are not going anywhere if you still insist on wearing them!'

'Happy?' he asks, reluctantly slipping off his glasses, revealing his large strikingly red veined eyes.

'Ecstatic (!),' I love it when he obediently follows my instructions, I wish Rakesh and Rishab would do the same. 'So where are you taking me tonight?'

'You'll see,' he says, unwilling to give much away.

After a few twists and turns we end up in a small by-lane. There doesn't seem to be a restaurant in sight as we now were right in the epicentre of an upmarket residential area. I look questioning at Veer. Veer smiles and leaps out and I find him holding the door out for me.

A few minutes later I find myself in the lounge of a small apartment. A maroon settee, with two mismatched cobalt blue cushions, covers much of the room. At least two hundred assorted candles and rose petals have been placed strategically on the lounge floor.

'You know we have some serious health and safety issues here! Is this your flat? How could you leave all this unattended?' Although the scene was as clichéd and cheesy as Veer's one-liners, I was trembling, it had become clear this setup was a subterfuge to seduce me. The late night meetings, the flirty text messages, surely I did have a clue I would find myself alone with Veer one day. Why was I using humour to bat the inexorable? Was I just about to embark on a treacherous path of adultery?

'Shhhhhhh.....you have no idea how long I've waited for this moment,' I felt his finger softly settle on my trembling lips. Why was I suddenly becoming aware of my Victorian-style granny underwear?

I could feel Veer's other hand on my shoulder blades and then I could feel it descend steadily on my back. As Veer inches closer into the glow of the candle light, I realise his eyes are locked into mine, our lips too close for comfort. The beat of my heart is almost deafening as I feel the softness of his lips against mine. He pulls me even closer to him and I feel his hot breath as he is about to consume me. I push him away with one mighty force.

'Veer! I wasn't ready for this set-up...I am a married woman!' I catch myself chanting about my marital status once again.

'Oh for God's sake, Natasha, don't I know that? Stop being such a prude. What's wrong with a bit of fun? We both know there is sizzling chemistry between us, why deny it?'

'Chemistry? I am thinking history here. Have you even given it a thought? The lives we may end up destroying in the process. You have a girlfriend and I have a husband and a child to think about. Rakesh doesn't deserve this.'

'Marry me,' Veer comes up with an instant solution to our complicated lives.

'I beg your pardon, did I just hear what I think I heard?'

'Yeah, if you want to make it legit... then marry me!'

This was an absurd declaration to make, even for Veer. I couldn't breathe, I needed to get my head around Veer's staged seduction, his unexpected proposition, things were moving way too fast. One minute it's all a bit of fun and the next minute it's about making a commitment.

As I turned to open the door, I could feel Veer's body press against mine. Several soft kisses burn my skin on the back of my neck, he strokes my hand gently murmuring into my ear 'Don't go, please don't leave me. I need you babe...'

Chapter Twenty Two

'Good morning passengers, this is your Captain Ian Russell speaking. We are due for departure shortly and will be reaching Mineta San Jose Airport at approximately...' the words that follow sound muffled as my mind buzzes with emotional thoughts.

I shut my eyes in the hope the recent memories would fade away but they come flooding back to me at breakneck speed. I didn't succumb to Veer's advances but I did take his proposition seriously. I left Veer on his own to savour the essence of scented candles and rose petals while I started building a new life with Veer and Rishab in my muddled head.

Was this destined to happen, was I really meant for Veer? I loved his dangerous recklessness, his laboured and contrived sense of humour, his delusional sexiness and his phenomenal cheesy overtures. He was so unconventional but yet so right. Was I falling in love with him or was I always in love with him? When I felt his hot breath on me, I was just as ready to ravish him as he was ready to consume me.

I had to keep my urges in check, I was someone's wife, mother, I couldn't possibly be leaping into someone's bed/ rose petal strewn floor without thinking about the devastating consequences. Some might say, for God's sake it's just one night of passion and a way to explore what might lie beyond. But for me with deep-rooted values instilled by my parents and a prude for a sister, I found the entire concept of adultery a bit slutty. Even if it was with someone I loved. How could I face Rakesh, Rishab, my parents and Tina? I couldn't do this to them, I wouldn't be able to live with myself!

However, I could finish with Rakesh and accept Veer's proposal and then re-ignite the passion respectably. That sounded like a water tight plan.

I made my way to Veer's flat. I had sent him a text to indicate I was coming to see him. This was also sent to ensure the coast was clear. Veer had just rolled out of bed and had made no effort to look like a prospective groom. He was working the 'grubby look', wearing an old T-shirt with a huge curry stain on it and shorts that was making a monumental effort to stay where it should, he greeted me with the same degree of enthusiasm as I would do with Maya.

He asked if I would like to have black coffee as he had run out of tea bags and milk.

The candles and petals had been cleared away. The place looked sombre without them.

I couldn't help but feel slightly unwanted for the first time, not sure if there was a lady visitor sprawled on his bed. I made several vain attempts to peer into his room and finally decided to bravely enter where no self respecting married woman would have gone. I was relieved to discover that he had been on his own. Why was I surprised?

The ambience didn't seem right to approach the subject of matrimony. But it had to be done. I had come bustling in with hopes, dreams, aspirations and images of the two of us walking into the sunset happily ever after and the whole shebang.

'Veer, about your proposition the other night...' I noticed Veer had begun to look edgy. He lit up a cigarette. He knew just how much I hate the smell of smoke and detested the fact that his cigarette got more attention than I did this time.

'What proposition?' Veer was dumbfounded with my query and I began to question myself if I had dreamt it all up.

'You, asking me to marry you...try not to look so shocked (!)' I snapped right back and struggled to keep the bitterness from my tone. The moment seemed surreal; it wasn't going the way I'd imagined.

'Oh! That! I was just messing, you didn't take me seriously, did you?' he looked amused and shrugged. He settled himself on the settee while I was left standing like a right lemon; he stretched his legs on a cane stool and took another puff from his ciggie.

I wasn't sure if I should have made him swallow his cigarette or thrown his hot black coffee over him. I didn't know what to make of his personality change, was this the same incorrigible Veer that I knew and loved? I fought back my tears; I was not going to let him enjoy this.

'Pardon me, Veer, you aren't suggesting I have a vivid imagination, are you? Wasn't it you that wooed me all these weeks, sending me flirty text messages, finally bringing me here and proposing marriage?'

I was shaking, I suppressed the urge to pick the ashtray next to Veer and try my shot putting skills. Rage was fuming within my soft belly.

He cleared his throat portentously and spewed the lines expertly liked he'd been in similar circumstances before.

'O Nuts, Nuts, my sweet vulnerable Nuts...it was all a bit of fun,' He lifted his head and looked directly at me. 'I find you very attractive, sure I do,' *Oh that's very charitable of you, asshole.* 'I can't deny that...but you've known all along Nazia and I are an item,' he wasn't lying, yes I did know that all along, but yet I had been so gullible. He'd played me so well.

I had to hand it to the guy, he was strategist – a strategic adulterer. With militant precision he had singularly devised his game plan. Except, after a quick impact assessment he would have deduced that his 'project' wasn't fit for purpose. As the chants of matrimony and commitment proved tiresome and had dramatically outweighed the benefits; he'd decided to abandon the kinky venture. Besides why would he want to lose Nazia? Where would he find another concurring partner who would agree to a polygamous relationship?

'We've been through so much, surely I can't give up all that!' With that declaration he took a lung exploding drag from his cancer stick.

I felt sick and my mouth felt dry. I couldn't imagine anyone could be so guiltless and uncaring, let alone my own friend, one whom I had been so fond of. Why would he have wanted to twist a knife in me like this? I couldn't blame it on alcohol because clearly he wasn't drunk.

'You are my sweetest friend,' he snorted as I seethed 'I was after a bit of fun but you got serious and spoilt the fun for me!'

'Veer, I am glad I saw this side to you, because all along you were this lost soul I needed to rescue and restore. I wanted to make up for all those years of pain that you endured with your parents splitting up and me choosing Rakesh over you. But now I know you have been a selfish, self-obsessed dickhead! And I hope to God you'll never find happiness as long as you live!' I roared.

I remember vaguely standing in silence for a while, studying his face, his body language, his blatant vile arrogance. There was no sense of remorse and I left behind a shell of man who I thought was my dearest friend and confidante. For the first time I felt I was in the presence of evil. He saw me as one of his twisted fantasies. Fifteen odd years has changed an endearing man into something I didn't recognise. Is this the price one pays for success? Tina was right there is another part to the glamour world that was dark and sinful.

How could I have got it so wrong? I remember vaguely staggering out of his flat and making it to my car, just.

I felt faint and tried not to pass out and tumble into a nearby ditch. I blinked away the dizzy spells as I gasped and fought back my tears. I reached for my phone and instinctively searched for Rakesh's number. He would make all the pain go away in a flash. Before it could start ringing at the other end, I realised what I had done. I hurriedly switched off the phone.

All our happy memories together came whooshing back. Our first kiss – which was not to be. My inexperienced Rakesh shut his eyes and misjudged the position of my features and went for my chin. He had prepped hard, watching English movies in the privacy of his room and practicing it with his pillow before the launch.

I was the first to know about his acceptance into medical college, his new job or any of his other momentous accomplishments. He gifted me with a second hand car when I'd secured my first job. He would have liked to buy me a new one, but couldn't afford it. He didn't want me using public transport as he was aware of my neurotic obsession with hygiene.

I have been stupid. So stupid. Rakesh has been a rock to me all these years. Propelled by the mere urge for passion, spontaneity and adventure, I was prepared to give the life Rakesh and I had built for ourselves, in a flash.

I sat behind the wheel for a few minutes before driving away from the lane I would never revisit in this lifetime.

With Rishab's school holidays fast diminishing I had to make a decision quick. Do I stay on in India or head back to America? I weighed my options. How was I going to live in the city which was full of memories, memories that I wished to put behind me? How was I going to face Rakesh? I would have to come clean with Rakesh about my encounter with Veer, he deserved to know the truth. How would a conservative and faithful man accept my foolishness? I would need to sit him down and say it's over and that he deserves better.

'Can't wait to see Dad... I've missed him.' Rishab comes to life as we are about to descend.

'I've missed him too, honey!' I say, ruffling his spikey hair.

Rakesh and Raghu stood at the arrival lounge beaming at the sight of us. I can't bring myself to hold Rakesh's grateful gaze. Rishab darts across the polished floor into the arms of his father. Raghu smiles at me indulgently as I hug him.

I find the house still standing which is a miracle in itself. I enter our house and find more surprises in store. The rooms, kitchen – all spotlessly clean. Exactly how I'd left them. I find Maya watching her Indian television programme soaking in the mother-in-law/daughter-in-law drama. She makes no attempt to tear her eyes away from the screen as she hears us walk in. Rishab flies up the stairs to reclaim his room and launch himself on his 'own' bed that he thought would never see. It is funny how one thing that makes home coming special is the sight of your own bed even though you may have slept in the most luxurious and scrumptious bed since you've been away.

As Rakesh and I enter our bedroom, Rakesh pulls me towards him and I surrender to a warm passionate hug. I can feel his warmth on my skin. He strokes my hair gently and plants numerous soft kisses on them. He smells clean citrusy fresh and the scenario becomes strangely familiar. Clichéd as it may seem, the mystery man of my dreams has been Rakesh all along!

'Rakesh, we need to talk.' I say huskily. I don't know where to begin.

'Hush baby...I know...I know about Veer. Tina has told me all about him,' he reveals.

Tina as it happened prided herself on being a family sleuth after stumbling upon one accidental cyber discovery. She supposedly read between the lines when I mouthed my concerns about my marriage and my vivid reaction when Veer's name was mentioned. She repaid her 'human smoke screen' debt by turning into one herself! Rakesh and Tina had 'worked in partnership' and had me under surveillance since the day I'd met up with Veer at Lou's Blues. Steve's sight-seeing itinerary would have been cleverly chalked out to allow her to be in two places at the same time, unless Steve was in with her the whole time! Stealthily, my crafty human smoke screen had followed me to all my furtive meetings with Veer...even to his flat. At one point she was going to burst into Veer's candle-lit flat like a secret undercover agent searching for suspects, had I stayed there longer than fifteen minutes.

'I have not been entirely blameless. Let's make a proper start. Just you and me this time,' Rakesh says as he lowers his mouth. I couldn't agree more.